AFTER WE FALL

A DARE WITH ME SERIES NOVEL

J.H. CROIX

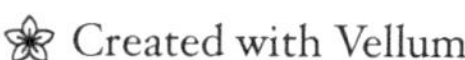 Created with Vellum

To my sweetest girl.

Sign up for my newsletter for information on new releases & get a FREE copy of one of my books!

http://jhcroixauthor.com/subscribe/

Follow me!
jhcroix@jhcroix.com
https://amazon.com/author/jhcroix
https://www.bookbub.com/authors/j-h-croix
https://www.facebook.com/jhcroix
https://www.instagram.com/jhcroix/

Chapter One

HARLEY

"Grant is totally hot," my friend Jodi said.

I almost spit out my coffee, sputtering, "What?"

"Oh, come on. Don't tell me you haven't noticed," she said, her tone sly.

Jodi was a childhood friend. She'd come up to Alaska for a visit and spent a week with us recently, and we were catching up on a call.

"Grant was hardly around when you were here. He's not around much in general," I added. That part was true. I hoped she didn't notice that I was dodging her comment.

"It's not like you have to see someone a lot to notice they're hot. Plus, you're avoiding my point. Don't you think he's hot?"

I let out a sigh. "Sure. Objectively speaking." I was relieved we were on the phone because my face was on fire.

"He's got that whole smoky gaze. Can you call a man a smoke show?" she teased.

I laughed. "I don't know."

Grant did, in fact, have smoky eyes. They were an

unusual glacial blue with a charcoal rim. As Jodi had pointed out, he *was* totally hot. That man was in some serious shape and didn't even work out.

I happened to be standing in my bedroom, where a full-length mirror was mounted on the door. Glancing at my own reflection, I bit back a sigh. I could've called myself curvy if I was feeling generous about it.

I enjoyed food. There was *a lot* of good food here where I lived.

Oblivious to my train of thought, Jodi added, "I think you two would be good for each other."

"What?!" I sputtered. "Grant can hardly stand me. Trust me, I don't think we'd be good for each other."

"It's like in elementary school. The kid who's the most annoying and picks on you totally likes you."

"Can we drop this topic, please?"

"I'm sure it's hard to ignore him since you have to live with him," she teased.

I gritted my teeth and ground out, "As if I didn't know."

She chuckled. "I'll drop it, but you getting all defensive only proves my point."

"Whatever."

"I'm really glad I got to come up there and see you. Thank you for inviting me," she said sincerely.

"Of course. I figure everybody should come to Alaska once. It was on my bucket list before Diego moved up here. Speaking of roommates, you could reconsider and move up here. I'm sure you can find a job."

"I appreciate the thought, but I don't think I could deal with winter there. I'm a born and bred Texas girl, and I like it hot."

I laughed. "Understood. The winters are cold. I'd be lying if I said anything otherwise."

"Thanks for being honest," she deadpanned.

We chatted a bit more, updating each other on the details of our lives. Just before we were about to end the call, Jodi teased, "Grant likes you!" in a singsong voice.

With a groan, I tapped the button to end the call. I'd already said goodbye. I didn't need to take her bait and argue the point again. Tossing my phone on the bed, I grabbed my laptop off the dresser and made myself comfortable propped against the pillows. My job was mostly online. I worked as a freelance graphic designer and also did medical transcription. I loved graphic design. Aside from my steady flow of online work, I also handled all of the marketing graphics for the outdoor resort where I lived. Sometimes I worked downstairs because I often had the house to myself.

My cheeks got hot again even though I was alone in my bedroom. Grant *was* hot and kind of cute. He was also a really nice guy. I didn't fall for nice guys. Relationships weren't my thing. No way would I risk ruining this sweet setup by letting anything happen with Grant. I had free room and board, awesome meals, and I lived near my brother.

I lived and worked at Walker Adventures, an outdoor resort in Alaska. It was just outside Diamond Creek, one of the coastal jewels of Southcentral Alaska. Diamond Creek was a beautiful little town nestled in the foothills of the mountains with the glittering waters of Kachemak Bay beside it.

My brother, Diego, was a pilot and flew for Walker Adventures. One of his best friends, Flynn Walker, owned the place. They'd been in the Air Force together. When I came up to visit, I ended up staying. My brother used to live in the staff house at the resort, but he'd fallen in love and moved out to live with his girlfriend. That left me here with Grant and Cat, who were Flynn's younger siblings.

Grant was busy, and he was gone a lot, which was a massive relief because I'd been crushing on him—hard —ever since I'd moved up here. I kept telling myself I would get over it. Unfortunately, my body was ignoring every memo I sent. I tried to be stern with myself. I even had a few mental knock-down, drag-out fights with my hormones. They were pretty powerful and had left my willpower feeling defeated.

I sighed aloud in the bedroom and tapped on my computer screen. I had some work to do on the website for Walker Adventures, so I might as well focus on that right now. We had plenty of business, but I wanted to up their website game. I'd started creating profiles for all the pilots. Of course, my naughty little index finger clicked on the tab that took me to Grant's profile.

Sweet hell. My pulse took off like a thoroughbred in a race.

There he was. Rugged and handsome with sharp, chiseled features. He looked a lot like his brother, Flynn. I clicked over to Flynn. Nothing, nothing. My pulse was all ho-hum.

I switched back to Grant. He had dark-blond hair and glacial-blue eyes with a charcoal rim, angled cheekbones, a straight blade of a nose, a square jaw, and full lips. I clicked back to Flynn. Still zero physical reaction. Flynn was happily married and deeply in love with Daphne. I didn't want to want Flynn. I really didn't, but if I could feel any spurt of *anything* with my hormones, then I wouldn't feel so crazy about Grant.

Jodi was right. Grant *was* hot. But she was wrong about him liking me. Although he was a nice guy, he treated me pretty much the way he treated his younger sister, Cat. I sighed again. I clicked out of Grant's profile, abandoning that project to work on something else.

Hours later, I was asleep in my bed, minding my own business. I didn't know what woke me up, but I came awake abruptly. My laptop had slid off my lap onto the mattress. I heard a sound, and then I could have sworn I heard Grant's voice. What the hell?

I'd fallen asleep in a pair of sweatpants and an old T-shirt. Rolling out of bed, I walked into the hallway. Grant's bedroom door was open, the lights were out, and there was no sign of him. I hurried down the stairs, worry percolating in my thoughts. I dashed out onto the porch when I heard more noise. The motion-activated porch light was already on. A giant bull moose was pawing the ground and snorting, all bossy-like.

"Grant?" I called.

"Yeah?" he returned, frustration evident in his tone.

"Are you okay?"

"For now. We need to chase this guy off."

I studied the moose, who was completely ignoring me. Glancing around, I saw the snow shovel propped in the corner of the porch. It wasn't winter, but the shovel had been waiting for its moment. I snagged it and banged it against the railing. The sound reverberated loudly. The moose stopped pawing the ground and turned to face me. Its antlers were illuminated by the porch light. A stab of fear galvanized me, and I banged the shovel again.

The moose took a step back, eyeing me warily. I jogged to the base of the stairs and picked up a rock. I threw it at him, hitting him in the rump. The moose snorted, turning once more to look at me. Another moment later, he seemed to decide it wasn't worth the trouble and loped off into the darkness.

"He's gone!" I called.

"I'm going to give it a minute to be safe," Grant answered.

He waited until the sound of the moose's hooves striking the ground faded. Meanwhile, I stood on the porch.

Grant approached in the darkness. Because my eyes were freaking annoying, I scanned him once he was within the circle of light cast by the porch. His gait had a slight hitch. Before I knew it, I was actually running off the steps.

"Grant! Are you okay?"

He stopped in front of me, and I looked up. He had a nasty scrape on his cheek and his shirt was torn. I could see blood staining the ragged fabric over his shoulder. "What happened?"

"The moose kicked me," he said with a shrug like it wasn't even a thing.

He stepped around me, walking up the steps and through the open door. I hurried after him.

"Grant!" I exclaimed as I slammed the door behind us.

He walked into the kitchen, grabbing a glass out of the cabinet and turning on the faucet to fill it with water. Seconds later, he gulped it down before he turned and looked at me. "I'm fine."

"You're bleeding!" I yelped.

"My face isn't too bad," he offered, lightly touching the scraped area.

"It's not your face. Obviously, your face got scraped."

"Yeah, that's when I fell," he interjected.

"It's your shoulder." I pointed at his bloody shoulder.

He glanced down, his eyes widening slightly. "Oh, shit. I didn't even notice that."

"Adrenaline will do that," I pointed out.

I crossed over to him. Manhandling him a little, I shoved him down in a kitchen chair.

"Let me get a look at that. You might need stitches."

"Oh, for fuck's sake. I do not need stitches, Harley," he muttered.

I started to pull apart the fabric but realized it was dirty. "Take your shirt off," I ordered.

Of all the things I *never* expected to say to Grant Walker.

He obliged, and I tried not to notice his muscled, bronzed chest with a smattering of amber hair. His shoulder was already swelling, and the cut was deep. "Is this where he kicked you?"

"I don't know. He charged me. It all happened really fast. I fell. I know I scraped my face on a rock or something. I probably cut my shoulder on something too."

"We need to clean this up. I think we should take you to the hospital."

"No. It's just a cut. The first-aid stuff is right in that cabinet." He nudged his chin toward the corner cabinet.

I hurried over, fetching a plastic bin containing bandages, antiseptics, and so on. Because this was Walker Adventures, the entire family and everyone working here were badass and outdoorsy. They risked their lives on the regular flying in the Alaskan skies. This was a seriously well-stocked first-aid kit.

"Let me clean it first. I'll use warm water and soap and then disinfect it."

A few moments later, I was eyeing the cut. It was clean, but it still looked terribly painful.

Grant glanced toward his shoulder. "Just put some butterfly bandages on it and then cover it with a larger bandage."

"You know, you don't have to be all tough. Some stitches wouldn't be a bad idea."

"I don't need stitches, Harley," he insisted.

I rolled my eyes. My heart was still racing from discovering he was injured, and I was anxious and worried. The scrape on his cheek was starting to swell. "It's going to look like somebody punched you in the face," I commented.

"I'll just tell them you did it," he returned with a wink and a quick grin. The very grin that sent my belly into somersaults on the regular and did so right now.

Despite his injured state, my hormones were disobedient.

Chapter Two

GRANT

Harley was a handful, and I wanted to kiss her. I'd wanted to kiss her for too damn long. But she was off-limits. Unfortunately, she was also my roommate. Fuck my life.

"Grant," she began. She actually wagged her finger at me. "I really think we should go to the hospital."

"I really think you should get the butterfly bandages out, pour peroxide or alcohol over it, and put the bandages on."

I wasn't thinking when I reached out and placed my hands on her hips to turn her around. "There's antibiotic ointment in the smaller container in the cabinet."

Fuck me. Her hips were soft, my fingers pressing into the lush give of her curves. Thank fuck I was sitting down because I was sporting a serious hard-on at this point. All over Harley, my friend's little sister. I had two younger sisters myself. I knew the rules. You were not supposed to fall for anybody's sister. Definitely not a younger sister.

Harley stepped away, marching back to that cabinet, her hips swinging with every step. She fetched the smaller container in question and returned, opening it. "Oh, I see. All right. I should use alcohol just because you won't take my advice," she muttered.

"Go for it."

She looked my way again and then shook her head. "No, that would be mean." She lifted the bottle of peroxide and dampened a cotton ball with it before gently dabbing it across the cut. I felt the bubble of the peroxide and a subtle sting, but it wasn't too bad.

She worked quietly, cleaning it thoroughly and dabbing antibiotic ointment on it before following my instructions to bandage it.

"That gash is three inches long. It's definitely going to leave a scar," she announced.

I glanced up at her. She'd been standing close to me, touching me this whole time, yet I'd been focused on what she was doing. It helped that the cut hurt. My shoulder was beginning to throb. But now, my awareness shifted abruptly, like the flick of a switch, to Harley—her glossy, almost black hair, her big green eyes, her sensual lips, and the way her nose tipped up at the end.

Her tongue darted out, swiping across her bottom lip. "How do you feel?" she asked.

My fingers itched to touch her. There was almost a vibration of sensation, the need was so intense.

Her eyes darkened, and I could see the rapid flutter of her pulse at the base of her throat. My heartbeat was drumming madly in my chest.

"Fine." My voice came out husky. I cleared my throat.

She smoothed her hand over the bandage again, checking to ensure the edges were pressed down.

"You should take some ibuprofen before you go to bed. It's going to be sore."

"It already is," I answered honestly.

Her eyes swung to mine again, blinking. In another second, she spun away, hurrying over to the cabinet by the sink where we kept a bottle of ibuprofen. "How many?" she asked.

"Two," I called in response.

She shook the bottle, dropping two pills in the center of her palm, and returned to me. Her fingertips brushed mine as she handed them over with another glass of water. I swallowed them quickly. Everything seemed loud. The sound of my throat moving was audible in the quiet kitchen. The clock went *tick, tock, tick, tock* where it was mounted on the wall above the stove. I didn't even realize I'd lost my internal battle of wills in trying to keep my hands to myself. Because I suddenly realized my palm was resting on her hip, just where it began to flare out below her waist.

Her breath hitched in her throat. "Grant?" Her voice held a barely-there hint of a question.

"Yeah?"

"What are you doing?"

I almost told her the truth—that I wanted to kiss her—but that was foolish and reckless. And *really* stupid. I gave her hip a light squeeze and a pat. "Thank you."

"For what?"

"Oh, for chasing the moose off with a shovel and a rock and bandaging my shoulder," I teased lightly, trying not to think about what her lips might feel like.

Pink crested high on her angled cheekbones. She stared at me. I sensed she knew I was dodging. At least I wasn't lying. I really was appreciative of her help.

"I'm sure you could have handled it yourself. You are Alaskan born and raised, after all."

I forced my hand to drop away from her hips even though I wanted to kiss her senseless. I shrugged. "Maybe I've had more encounters with moose than you, but they're unpredictable."

She snorted as she turned away and quickly gathered up the first-aid supplies. "Maybe so, but that's the closest I've been to one."

"Really? You've been here over a year."

She shrugged. "I know, but I've only seen them from a distance. He seemed scary tall."

I let out a sharp laugh. "He was pretty tall. I think you had a better view than I did, though, since you were on the porch. As soon as I heard him coming, I tried to get the hell out of the way and got kicked instead. Moose are big in general."

"Do I need to worry about him coming back?" she asked, looking genuinely concerned.

Then she went and bit her bottom lip, a habit of hers I was fairly convinced served solely to torture me. My cock throbbed, and I curled my hand on the edge of the chair. "Maybe, but we always need to keep our eye out for moose. They're around a lot."

"I just make a lot of noise, right?"

"Yeah. Like I've told you before, they're nearsighted. You want to make sure they hear you before they see you. By the time they see you, it might be too late. I kind of zoned out when I was walking back."

"From a night at the bar?" she asked.

"Sure. Is that a problem?"

"No. Of course not. It's your life, not mine."

"You could go out with me sometimes," I pointed out.

"Why?" Her sharp tone, the arch of her brow, and the skepticism in her gaze needled me.

"Why not? We're roommates. We're friends, right?"

"Sure, but I don't really do bars. Plus, no offense, but I'm not up for playing your wing-woman while you go out and hit on women."

I rolled my eyes. "I just like to knock back a beer or two and relax."

She shrugged. "Plus, we're only sort of roommates."

"What does that mean?"

She crossed her arms, tapping the toe of one socked foot on the floor. "Because you're not always here. You often stay out the whole night when you go out."

Harley and her opinions. I shook my head. "You know I have friends. I usually just crash with them. I don't get around the way you imply."

"I'm not implying anything." Her arms dropped. "Whatever. I'm glad you're okay. Good night," she said tartly.

Her sweet, curvy hips were a magnet for my eyes when she marched past me. She might as well have had a string attached to me. My head turned, watching as she strode briskly through the wide archway out of the kitchen into the living room and up the stairs. Her hips swayed temptingly with every step.

"Fuck," I muttered under my breath.

Once I heard her bedroom door close, I stood, straightening my jeans. I was relieved she was out of sight because my arousal was visible. Fuck. I would have to take a cold shower to deal with this.

Chapter Three

GRANT

"What the hell happened to your face?" Flynn asked. My older brother took a swallow of his coffee, arching a brow in question.

"A moose happened to his face is what I heard," Daphne, his wife, offered.

"A moose charged me in the dark when I was walking back to the house last night. He kicked me and knocked me to the ground. My face looks worse, but my shoulder hurts." I rolled it carefully. "Ouch."

"What happened to your shoulder?"

"That I don't know. When the moose charged and kicked, I fell. I'm not sure if it was the moose or the ground that got it. Harley cleaned it up and bandaged it last night."

Daphne clucked as she approached me, her eyes skating over my face. "Are you okay to fly?"

"Of course," Flynn replied in unison with me.

Flynn chuckled. "It's a good story for the tourists."

Daphne put her hands on her hips. "Why would you say that?" she demanded, spinning to face him.

Flynn's grin stretched, his blue eyes twinkling with a sly gleam.

"Because they love that shit. Bear and moose encounters are great stories."

Daphne huffed. "My one moose encounter up close and personal was enough."

"Which one was that?" I asked as I poured myself a cup of coffee.

"When I was here for my trip, I went for that hike down by the beach that Nora told me about. When I returned, there was a moose on the path near the parking area. It didn't do anything, but I had to take a detour. That's when I fell into that devil's club. That stuff is mean, and I never thought I'd describe a plant as mean." She sighed, and her cheeks went a little pink when she glanced at Flynn.

That trip was when Flynn and Daphne fell in love. Thank God for that. My older brother was *way* less grumpy than he used to be with her around. She took the edge off him.

"Well, now you know to avoid devil's club," I offered.

Daphne rolled her eyes as she got busy at the stove. I took a swallow of my coffee and glanced toward the windows. We were in the kitchen at the main lodge of Walker Adventures. I remembered this place before Flynn returned from the Air Force to take care of Nora and Cat. And me, I suppose. I'd started college at the time. I'd mostly been partying, relieved to be away from my dad. I'd missed my mom, but she'd only been able to provide a small haven away from the chaos my father created from bouncing in and out of our lives at his leisure. He and my mom had started this place, but we'd come a long way from those days.

My dad had been a pilot, and he'd had this idea that he would do this guiding business with my mom. This kitchen had been under construction, and we didn't even have any guest rooms. My dad had passed away, and then my mom barely held it together before passing away from an undiagnosed genetic heart problem. Nora had been in high school, and Cat had just started middle school.

Thank God for Flynn. He'd been in the Air Force and had left to come home as soon as he could. I'd immediately returned from college to try to hold the threads of our family together until he could get here.

At the time, the court had been concerned that nineteen was too young for me to be my sisters' guardian. I could do the basics for them, but I sure as hell couldn't have done what Flynn did. When he returned, he'd assumed the role of father figure to all of us. He had a different father than the rest of us, one he'd never known. He'd worked night and day to turn this half-assed idea into a full-fledged outdoor resort and flight business catering to Alaskan tourists.

I let my eyes scan the space. This kitchen was nice with a beautiful view. A long table was situated in front of the windows for the guests and us. A fancy-looking industrial-style kitchen sat at the back of the large room with a counter encircling the working space. I rounded the counter, slipping my hips onto a stool, and watched as Daphne got started.

She made breakfast for the staff and guests every day. We had seven pilots now. Flynn, me, Nora, and Flynn's friends from the Air Force, who were all like family—Elias, Gabriel, Diego, and Tucker. We also had a little help from a local pilot who took the evening flights one day a week for us and pitched in with a little extra help here and there if somebody was sick or out of town. This lodge had transformed from a half-completed single story into three stories with guest rooms occupying the top two floors. There was also the staff house, which was just me, Cat, and Harley these days. Harley was Diego's younger sister. Everybody else had gradually moved out of the staff house one by one as they fell in love.

My mind spun back to last night. I was an early riser either way, but I'd woken up earlier than usual because my shoulder hurt like hell. Stiff and sore, I'd knocked down some ibuprofen and taken a quick shower before bolting from the house. I'd still dreamed about Harley last night after finding a quick release in the shower. Fuck me.

We'd never laid a finger on each other until last night when she cleaned up my shoulder. I gave my head a shake, turning my attention to Daphne. "What's for breakfast?"

"Egg casserole with ham and cheese. It'll be delicious. That's already baking. I'm also making waffles for anyone who wants them." She adjusted the heat on something she was stirring on the stove.

"What's that?"

"I'm making syrup."

I smiled over at her. "Thank God you're here."

Her hazel eyes twinkled as she smiled back at me. "Yeah?"

"Uh, yeah. We get the best food ever because you're a kick-ass chef."

Daphne was the real deal when it came to being a chef. She'd signed up for a month here. She was originally from Atlanta and came out to Alaska after a personal tragedy when her young son died from some kind of brain cancer. She stayed because our cook at the time quit. Flynn wasn't the best boss, but it was no big loss.

With Daphne here, she offered to help, and then she stayed. By that point, she and Flynn were half in love, if not entirely in love.

"Aside from the best food ever, you make life better for Flynn and all of us," I added emphatically.

Flynn grinned over at me and winked. "Damn straight." He lifted a hand, resting it on her shoulder as he leaned over to press a quick kiss on her cheek. He knew not to interrupt her too much when she was cooking. She smiled up at him. The sunlight angling through the windows cast a gold shimmer on her auburn hair, which was twisted in a braid and pinned on top of her head.

"I love it here," she said simply. "Now, do you want waffles along with the egg casserole?"

"Hell, fucking yes," Flynn said.

"What kind of syrup are you making there?" I asked.

"Blueberry. These are from the wild blueberries on the property."

"Seriously?"

Daphne grinned. "Cat and I have fallen into the habit of grabbing a quart jar whenever we go out. There are tons of wild raspberries too, so I'm going to make raspberry vinegar."

"What are you gonna do with that?" Flynn asked.

"Oh, that is delicious on pancakes."

"Really?"

Daphne nodded. "Yep."

"Sign me up," I said.

"How many waffles do you want?" she asked. She turned on the waffle maker.

A few minutes later, Flynn and I were eating at the

counter when the back door into the kitchen opened. It led from the back hallway where most of the staff came in. Harley appeared with her brother, Diego, right behind her.

"Hey, man, what are you doing out here?" I called.

"I came for breakfast. Gemma's doing her early morning yoga classes now, so I get up early."

"You just want Daphne's food," Harley said as she grinned up at him.

Diego shrugged. "Always good to see you, sis."

My body tightened when she stopped at the corner of the counter. Diego glanced over.

"What the hell happened to your face? Did you punch him?" he asked, glancing at Harley.

She grinned. "No. I would not punch him. He encountered a moose."

"Ah." Diego nodded. "That'll make a good story for the customers."

Daphne rested a hand on her hip, pointing the spatula at Diego. "Seriously? You guys are using his injuries for business."

Diego shrugged. "Whatever. People love that shit about Alaska—moose, bears, sea lions, all fodder for stories."

"I'll take the moose over the bear," Gabriel said as he came in, hearing the tail end of the conversation. "Ooh, you tangled with a moose," he added as soon as his eyes landed on my face.

"Yeah. Took me off guard last night. I think my face hit a rock, but my shoulder's worse."

"His shoulder looks like hell," Harley offered as she slipped her hips on a stool toward the end of the counter and sipped her coffee. "I had to bandage it, butterfly bandages and everything. I still think you need stitches."

I shook my head, and Daphne let out a huff. "Do I need to take you to the doctor?"

"No, I'm fine. I swear. I checked it this morning."

Gabriel sipped the coffee he'd just poured and eyed me. "Gonna be sore. You flying today?"

"Of course. It's Saturday. We're booked solid," I pointed out.

"We're booked solid every day. It's freakin' summer," Diego retorted.

"What's for breakfast?" Gabriel asked.

"Egg casserole and waffles," Daphne replied.

We fell into the easy banter characteristic of living and working here. I loved my job. I loved that Flynn had hustled to finish building this place and made it something for all of us. I loved flying planes, and I loved my family and friends. I couldn't ask for anything better. The only thing that felt odd was realizing that everybody else was paired up except for me, Harley, and my youngest sister Cat.

I couldn't even distract myself anymore. I wasn't about to admit it to anyone, but I had it bad for Harley, and I couldn't do a damn thing about it.

Speaking of Harley, her older brother Diego slipped his hips onto the stool beside me. He took a long swallow from his coffee before glancing at me. "How've you been? I haven't seen you in a week or so."

"Nah, our schedules weren't in sync, and you didn't come out for yoga class last week," I pointed out.

Diego chuckled. "I know. Gemma gave me some hell for that. I landed late for my last flight because somebody was delayed for a doctor's appointment. I wasn't going to leave without them."

"I'd have done the same thing," I offered with a shrug.

Aside from flying tourists, we ferried local residents from the various villages nearby to and from Diamond Creek and sometimes farther distances. On occasion, the weather could throw a wrench into timing and plans.

"The staff house must feel pretty spacious these days," Diego commented, glancing back and forth between Harley and me.

"It's three of us with Cat there now," I offered. "Don't even know what to do with all that space."

"Well, I'm not going to suggest that Harley fall in love because she's my little sister, so I guess it's your turn next," he teased.

I held a hand up. "I'm *not* falling in love."

I might have a serious case of lust for Harley, but love with anyone was out of the question. I couldn't imagine it for myself. My parents had been a terrible example of a relationship. My father had been the human equivalent of a ping pong ball, bouncing in and out of our lives while having affairs, doing his own thing, and barely contributing financially to the family. My mom had scraped by year after year. We'd all loved her. She'd been solid as a rock emotionally in many ways, but she seemed to have made the choice to ignore our father's treatment of her. As a kid, I learned nobody was there for you when it came to relationships. I figured I would just live the single life. It was easier that way. I had a good place to live, a sweet job that I loved, and friends and family who mattered.

This lust for Harley would pass. It had to. She had been here for over a year now. At first, I'd just thought she was cute. Since then, the tension I felt trying to ignore my desire for her only ratcheted up. I still wasn't sure what she thought of me, but I knew it was a bad plan for us to be involved.

Diego would probably kick my ass if he even knew

my train of thought, so it was pointless to contemplate.

"We should turn the extra bedrooms into guest rooms," Diego commented.

"Nah, man. I like having somewhere I can just relax," I offered.

Harley shook her head. "No. We can use the extra bedrooms for family and friends who want to visit. Maybe we should move our weekly staff dinners out there."

"I'm not cooking in that kitchen," Daphne called over.

Flynn chuckled. "And we would never make you do that."

"What's wrong with that kitchen?" I asked, genuinely curious.

"Nothing. I'm comfortable here, and I have all my things in this kitchen," she explained.

"We have the basics," I replied.

"Enough for you to handle basic meals," she replied.

"Hey, I can do more than that," I protested.

Just then, another voice called out, "No, you can't."

I glanced over to see my youngest sister, Cat, coming into the kitchen.

I grinned. "Fair enough."

Cat had moved into the staff house recently. Fortunately, she didn't drive me crazy anymore. We needled each other here and there because we were siblings, and that was what we did. Daphne had taught Cat how to cook, and now she was a *seriously* good cook.

"It's actually kind of nice having Cat at the house," I commented, glancing over at Flynn.

"Yeah?"

"She makes us extra snacks."

He grinned. "Are you keeping an eye on her?"

"Oh my God," Cat groaned. She narrowed her eyes at Flynn when she stopped beside Daphne as she tied an apron around her waist. "Waffles?" she asked.

Daphne nodded. "I'm cooking down the syrup."

"I'll mix up some more batter," Cat replied.

"Okay, so no staff dinner, but we could have card night out at the staff house," I added.

Daphne rolled her eyes. "I think we should have card night over here. It used to be a guy thing."

"Yeah, they stopped when I moved in," Harley interjected. "Let's start hosting it once a week."

"Works for me." I glanced over at Harley. The second her eyes met mine, it felt as if a sizzle zipped through the air between us.

Chapter Four

HARLEY

"What do you mean? Like that?" Gemma asked, clicking on a button on her computer screen.

"Just like that," I confirmed.

"Oh, well that's easy." Her eyes twinkled when she smiled over at me. "Do you really think I need a website?"

"Yes. That way, new people can find you, and customers can pay online. It's much easier. I promise."

"Thank you for doing this for me." She brushed her honeyed curls away from her cheeks.

"It's no big deal. You're family."

Gemma grinned over at me before glancing at Daphne. "She's the best almost sister-in-law I could ask for."

"Same," I returned as Daphne nodded in agreement.

Gemma, with her curls and blue eyes, was perfect for my brother. She was a soft edge to him. As a yoga teacher with a warm and kind personality, she was a good counterpart to his gruff but soft heart. Diego loved hard, and he deserved someone like Gemma.

I leaned back. "Let me finish up the back end."

I slid the laptop across the table to me. Her website was pretty simple with a basic about page for her and a calendar for her yoga classes. It allowed people to select times and sign up and pay right there.

"People can still pay when they show up for class, but this way, it's all set up in there for you. The system automatically tracks it and does your monthly accounting."

"Oh, that's amazing." She pressed her palm to her chest, letting out a sigh. "This is going to make it so much easier for me."

"That was the plan," I replied with a grin.

She leaned back in her chair, smiling. "Thank goodness for you. I'm not that tech savvy. There's no way I could set up a website."

"I got you on this. I'll make it so you can update it on your own if you'd like, but I will always do it if you need my help."

"Thank you. I will probably never update it unless you tell me I need to."

Cammi, a friend and the owner of Misty Mountain Café where we were meeting, approached, and replied to Gemma's comment, "She made my website too. I'm not updating it without her help."

She stopped by our table, smiling at us. "How's it going, ladies?"

"Good. You weren't here when we came in," Daphne replied.

"I had to run to the bank because we were short on cash for change. I have to get back in the habit of stopping by the bank almost daily during the summer."

Daphne let out a sigh. "That is one thing I don't mind not worrying about."

Cammi snagged an empty chair from a nearby table and sat down with us. "What do you mean?"

"Not worrying about all the cash," Daphne replied. "I love being the chef at the lodge. I just cook for the guests and staff. I don't have to handle bills or tips or anything."

Cammi grinned. "Ah." She owned this café along with Red Truck Coffee. Between the two businesses and recently having twins, she was busy, especially in the summer months when tourists descended on Alaska. "I don't mind it. I love the hustle and bustle."

"It's perfect for your personality. You're like a ray of sunshine," Daphne said earnestly.

Cammi burst out laughing. "A ray of sunshine?"

"Absolutely," a low male voice intoned.

We all glanced over to see Elias, Cammi's husband, and another one of the pilots at Walker Adventures, approaching our table. He leaned down and pressed a lingering kiss on Cammi's cheek. Her cheeks were flushed pink by the time he straightened.

"Sunshine is a good thing." He rested his hand at the base of her neck, squeezing lightly. "You're not behind the counter?"

"No, I'm having lunch with my friends," she said with a saucy smile.

He grinned. "Good. I'll go get my coffee then."

"Are you staying?" she asked as she swiveled around when he began to turn away.

"Don't have time, babe. Just grabbing a coffee. I have a flight." He glanced at his watch. "Oh, shit. I gotta hurry."

"Bye! I'll pick up the twins on the way home later." She blew him a kiss as he jogged to the counter.

When she turned back, Daphne smiled indulgently at her. "You have made Elias one happy man."

"I love him, so it's mutual," Cammi said simply.

"How's working and having twins going for you?" Daphne asked.

Cammi's smile was wry. "We're making it work, and I'm so grateful we have friends to help with daycare. Today, they're with Susie's mom. Everyone tells me life is just hectic with babies, and it is. I don't mind, and Elias is a big help."

"You know, I got his old room at the staff house. I didn't even really know him before you two were together. Rumor has it he used to be on the grumpy side," I commented.

"He was very mysterious," Cammi said, lowering her voice, her eyes glinting with mischief.

Daphne chuckled. "He wasn't mysterious at all. He had a crush on Cammi forever."

"He'd only been here for four years," Cammi protested.

"Okay, forever as long as he lived here," Daphne corrected.

Cammi laughed before letting out a soft sigh. She slid her eyes to me. "I think it's your turn."

"Excuse me?"

Daphne grinned. "Your turn to fall in love."

"Oh, no, no." I held a hand up, shaking my head swiftly. "No way."

"I said no way to love too," Daphne interjected. "I came to Alaska figuring I would never be in a relationship again." She held up her hands and let them fall.

I sighed. "You know, it would be easier to sell if I'd known either of you before you were ridiculously whipped. You have Flynn wrapped around your little finger." I gestured to Daphne. "And Elias worships the freaking ground you walk on." I waved toward Cammi. "I'm not like either one of you."

"What do you mean?" Daphne pressed, her eyes narrowing.

"I don't know how to explain it, but I'm not the kind of woman guys fall for."

"You haven't even dated since you've been here, and you've been here over a year," Gemma said.

"Yeah, I don't want to date. I am great at being single," I said firmly. "Hell, my last boyfriend Joe screwed my roommate. I walked in on that."

"You mentioned that, but honestly, you don't seem that upset about it," Gemma added.

I laughed a little. "No, not really. I was planning to break up with him anyway. I learned two things: She was a shitty roommate, and I had a good reason to break up with him. He's already cheated on her too."

"Comes around, goes around," Gemma said, nodding sagely.

"Did you really swear off relationships forever?" Cammi pressed.

I shrugged. "I'm kind of opinionated, and it's possible I might be difficult to deal with."

"Difficult?" Cammi looked puzzled.

"Outspoken, blunt. I'm not great at sucking up to guys," I explained.

"Neither are we," Daphne replied.

"Yeah, but you have a softer touch than me. I feel like I'm all sharp edges."

"I think you're just trying to find excuses," Gemma commented.

That was true, but I wasn't about to fess up to that.

"Maybe you don't want to be in a relationship, but ruling it out for no good reason is kind of silly," Daphne commented.

I bit back a sigh, and my heart twisted sharply. I

knew she had a point, and thinking about my emotional resignation when it came to relationships tended to remind me how much I wanted a family. I loved kids. Fiercely. Babies were the cutest. They smelled good. They were chubby. Their skin was soft, and they were magic.

Yet I just didn't have the best luck with relationships. I was almost thirty, and it felt like my biological clock was on fire. Even though I knew better intellectually, that's just how it felt.

"Maybe someday," I said nonchalantly. Just then, my heart fluttered oddly, and I felt my pulse race. I ignored it.

Daphne looked at me quietly. I loved Daphne. I hadn't known her for all that long, but she was sort of a mother hen, always taking care of everyone. She wanted everyone she loved to be happy. She seemed to have decided that meant finding their person.

"Maybe I don't want to find my person," I said, lifting my chin a little. "Maybe I'll be that single girl who lives a bold life."

Cammi cast me one of her sunny smiles, reaching over to give me a side hug. "Of course, you will."

Chapter Five

HARLEY

That night, I glanced over at Cat and Grant sitting on opposite sides of the sectional, bickering over what to watch. I was at a small table where I often worked on my laptop in the evenings.

"Just pick something, or I'll be the tiebreaker," I called over.

Cat glanced at me "What do you want to watch? Let's vote."

I shook my head quickly. "Surely you two can solve this. When it comes to television, you two turn into ten-year-olds."

Grant narrowed his eyes before he burst out laughing. That was the thing about him. He was a pretty easygoing guy, which made him all that much more attractive. I still hadn't been able to put the sight of his bare chest out of my mind.

"Do you want to play cards?" Cat asked.

"Why did card night stop out here?" I asked.

"Because we're the only people left," Grant said dryly.

"Are we not worthy of card night?" Cat countered.

"No, but we have to invite everybody over," Grant pointed out. "You should do girls' night cards," he added as he leaned back into the couch cushions.

"It used to be mostly guys, right?" I asked.

"Well yeah. Until you got here, it was all guys. Nora stayed here for a while, but then she built her cabin and moved out because she got sick of all the guys."

"How many of you were here?"

Grant lifted a hand, counting on his fingers. "Well, there was me, Gabriel, Elias, Tucker, and Diego, so there were five of us."

"But there aren't five bedrooms," I pointed out.

"Yeah. Tucker and Diego shared the biggest bedroom for a while."

"Really?" Cat asked.

"Yeah, didn't you notice there used to be two twin beds? We turned it into a pool room when only three of us were left," he explained.

Cat snickered. "Such a guy house. No wonder Nora wanted to move out."

"It was totally a guy house," Grant replied with a shrug.

"Let's invite all the girls out soon," I offered.

She squealed. "I'm in. I'll make appetizers."

"Perfect," I replied.

Grant grinned between us. "I guess that'll be one of my nights out then."

"You're always out," Cat said sharply.

"Why do you care?" he countered.

"I don't," Cat retorted.

Cat tossed a throw pillow in his direction. They quieted and settled on a comedy show while I continued to tap away on my laptop, adjusting some things on the website I was working on for another business in downtown Diamond Creek. When I had decided to come up here on a whim, I'd honestly thought most of my business would be online clients from a distance. While that did keep me busy, I had lots of local business. People here definitely wanted to support local businesses, and I benefited from that.

Hours later, I was alone in the living room. Grant and Cat had gone to bed. I tended to be a night owl. I also had a tendency to be an early riser. In short, I didn't sleep well. I had been fighting off a sense of restlessness all day. It had been an innocent enough conversation earlier, but Daphne and Cammi had gotten under my skin with their heartwarming teasing about falling in love. I didn't want to care. I also didn't want to be crushing on Grant because that was freaking annoying. With a sigh, I tapped the save button and powered down my laptop before closing it.

I stood to walk into the kitchen to get something. Abruptly, my breath became short, and my heartbeat felt funny. It felt as if the beats were out of order and skipping between too fast and too slow. Moments later, I was gasping for air and found myself on the floor beside the couch. I didn't have a clear idea of how I ended up there.

"Harley?" Grant's voice reached me from the base of the stairs.

I looked over, my thoughts were muddled and fuzzy. "Yeah?"

He crossed the room swiftly in long strides, kneeling beside me. "What the hell happened? You fell."

I didn't normally sit down in the middle of the floor like this, but I wanted to argue the point. The next thing I knew, he was checking my pulse, and I was trying not to get pissed off.

"I feel fine," I insisted.

"Did you faint? Have you eaten today? Your pulse feels okay."

"It's fine. I'm fine." I was sort of lying because internally, I was freaking right the hell out.

"I think we should get you up on the couch for a few minutes."

"Oh my God. You do not need to monitor me," I said.

Grant didn't care how I felt. "Deal with it."

A few minutes later, we were both sitting on the couch. He'd fetched me a glass of water. I thanked him earnestly because I *had* needed the water. I was mentally trying to figure out what lie I would make up to get out of this.

"I think you're right. My blood sugar must have been low," I offered in response to something he'd said moments earlier.

He was sitting a little too close for my comfort. Between checking my temperature and running me through questions to rule out a concussion, my comfort level had been obliterated.

"Dear God, you're so annoying," I said when he reached for my wrist to check my pulse again.

"We're all trained in first responder stuff because we fly in the middle of fucking nowhere half the time. If something happens, we have to be able to handle the basics."

"I know," I finally said. "But I'm fine. I'm right here. I'm not in the middle of nowhere."

Grant arched a brow, and I rolled my eyes. "Okay, I guess we kind of are, but you're here. We're in a house."

"Do you have a doctor here?"

"No."

I sighed. That was another small problem. I *should*

be seeing a doctor, but I didn't want to discuss that. Not with Grant. For the first time ever, I decided to distract myself by actually enjoying how he looked all up close and personal with the chiseled lines of his face, the hint of stubble gracing his jaw, and his sexy eyes.

He narrowed his gaze. "You should have a regular doctor. Hang on." He reached for his phone on the coffee table. "That's why I came downstairs. I forgot my phone."

"You need your phone when you sleep?"

He shrugged. "When I can't sleep, I play word games. It puts me to sleep real quick."

I couldn't help but laugh at that. Another moment later, my own phone vibrated where it sat nearby on the coffee table. "What did you send me?"

"Dr. Quinn Haynes. He's a great guy. He runs the family practice in Diamond Creek. We all go to him."

"Mmm. How's your shoulder?" I asked when I saw him turn and wince slightly.

"Much better. It's still sore, but it's definitely better."

"I'm glad you're okay."

"Yeah, me too. Thank you again."

"What for? Chasing the moose off with a shovel and a rock?"

"Yeah," he said, flashing a quick grin.

It felt like the air heated around us. As I said, he was *right* there beside me. I didn't know if it was just me or if he avoided me as well, but I was usually careful not to let myself get too close to Grant.

Now, my belly flipped with tingles radiating through my body. My heart raced, although it was for all the wrong reasons this time. As he looked down at me, I made a foolish but crucial decision.

I lifted a hand, dragging my fingertip along his jawline. "Just so you know, Grant, you're kind of hot."

"Excuse me?" His voice came out husky, and butterflies tickled my belly.

If I'd been standing, my knees would've given out. I felt all melty inside. I could be a bold girl when I wanted, so I leaned up, pressing a kiss right where my fingertips had just been.

I drew back, staring at him, daring myself and daring him. In another second, his head was dipping down as I leaned up. The second our lips met, it felt as if flames burst to life between us.

Grant muttered something, then angled his head sideways, fitting his mouth over mine. Oh hell, Grant just had to go and be an amazing kisser. His tongue swept boldly into my mouth, and I gasped. His hand slid into my hair, angling my head to the side.

He was all commanding, yanking the control right out of my hands. I had no idea how long we kissed, but a sound snapped into my awareness, and we broke apart. I reflectively glanced over, realizing Cat had just walked from her bedroom into the bathroom. We were both gasping for air and staring at each other.

"What the fuck, Harley?" he rasped.

"What?" I returned, straightening. "I wanted to kiss you. And don't lie. You wanted to kiss me too."

Grant blinked before running a hand through his hair as he let out a ragged sigh. "Fuck."

He stood to walk upstairs, spinning back to say, "Call the doctor."

Chapter Six

GRANT

I stared at the ceiling, but there wasn't much to see. The ceiling was plain white with shadows cast across it from the moonlight falling through the windows. It offered nothing for distraction.

My mind kept repeating the vivid recollection of kissing Harley, which sent a jolt of heat sizzling through me with each loop in my thoughts. I'd gone and done the stupidest thing ever and fucking kissed Harley.

"She kissed me first," I whispered aloud in the room. "She did."

You're just trying to make excuses.

It was mutual.

It doesn't really matter.

Who made the first move?

It was incremental.

You met her halfway.

My critical mind taunted me. Fuck me. I bunched the sheets in my fist, squeezing as if I could eliminate the energy coursing through my system. I refused, I absolutely refused, to give in and find my release to the mere moments-old memory of the feel of her lips underneath mine.

As a result, when I woke up the next morning, I was cranky as hell. I'd slept like shit. And I *still* couldn't stop thinking about Harley.

Resigned, I took care of matters in the shower out of pure desperation. Even though it was safe to say I didn't pray often, I tossed a little prayer to the universe, hoping Harley had already left the house. I didn't like to think of myself as a coward, but I wasn't really up for facing her this early.

After my shower, I leaned forward, checking out the wound on my shoulder in the mirror. It was healing up nicely. Despite her protestations, Harley had done a good job with the butterfly bandages. It was sealed and just sore now. The entire surface of the skin around the cut was bruised. I rolled my shoulder, testing the soreness. I brushed my teeth quickly, then considered shaving as I ran my fingers along the stubble on the side of my jaw. I decided against it when I glanced at my watch because I had just enough time to rush to the lodge and grab breakfast. That would get me to the airport on time for my first flight of the day.

I dressed quickly, letting out a quick sigh when I saw Harley's bedroom door open and the room empty. She always made her bed. When I jogged downstairs, the house was silent. Cat was gone too.

The air was cool when I stepped outside and jogged from the staff house to the main lodge. The sun was making its brisk climb into the sky, and it wasn't even seven o'clock yet.

A few minutes later, I walked through the back door into the kitchen and was assailed with the aroma of fresh cinnamon rolls. Cat was pulling them out of the oven and smiled over at me. "Your favorite!" she called.

"You know it," I answered.

I turned to grab a mug out of the cabinet nearby and pour myself some coffee. I felt the hairs rise on my neck as I set the coffee pot back and knew Harley had come in. I steeled myself as I glanced over my shoulder. She was walking through the archway from the front entrance. She paused to say something to her brother, Diego, reminding me with blinding clarity why I never, *never*, never should have kissed her last night.

Daphne appeared at my side with a fresh cinnamon roll on a small plate. "Just for you," she offered, her eyes twinkling.

"Ah, personal service. Thank you."

"Well, the minute I put them on the main table"— she angled her head in the direction of the table in front of the windows where guests were eating— "they'll be gone."

As soon as she handed the plate to me, she whisked away, buzzing about the kitchen like a little bee. I sat down at the counter, making quick work of the cinnamon roll. When Harley passed by and her eyes caught mine, I nodded in greeting. That was it.

Diego sat down beside me, casting me an easy grin. "Morning. You look like you're in a hurry."

I finished chewing the last bite of the cinnamon roll and took a swallow of coffee before replying, "I am. I had just enough time to get over here before I beat feet and get out to fly."

"Oh, that's right. You've got some early flights this morning. I'm sure I'll see you out there. Fly safe," he said as I stood.

"You do the same." I gulped the last of my coffee

and called out my goodbyes, thanking Daphne and Cat for breakfast.

I was so busy trying not to look around and collide with Harley's gaze again that I didn't realize she'd gone into the back hallway to use the bathroom. My hand was on the doorknob of the bathroom when it turned underneath, and she came walking out. I jumped back as if struck by lightning.

"Uh, hey," I said quickly.

Her eyes searched mine. I thought I saw a hint of uncertainty flickering there.

"Good morning," she said in a prim and proper tone.

I mumbled a greeting before I rushed past her into the bathroom. It felt like my elbow was on fire where it brushed against her arm. I practically slammed the door shut, then took a deep breath before locking it. Fuck me.

Chapter Seven

GRANT

"Hey, Grant," Layla said in a singsong voice.

Layla had long glossy brown hair and big blue eyes. Layla, who I'd spent more than one night with. Layla, who had no problem with a sort of friends-with-benefits arrangement. Sort of because our friendship was entirely superficial.

"Hey," I said as I turned, actually hoping I'd experience a little jolt of anticipation at seeing her.

Nothing, fucking nothing. No reaction. Nothing.

When I realized she was waiting expectantly, I added, "I don't usually see you out this way."

Which was entirely true. My friendship with Layla was limited to the boundaries of seeing her at local bars and, on occasion, spending the night with her. She was fun and easy to be with and had no expectations. There was just one problem now: that very thing that I looked for with her was something I didn't want anymore.

Harley had become too much of a distraction months before that stupid kiss last night.

"I don't usually come out here," Layla said, "but I

have some friends visiting. I told them the perfect thing was one of those flightseeing trips. I wouldn't do it with anybody other than Walker Adventures. Lucky for us, you're our pilot today."

Her tone was light and flirty. I managed to smile. "Ah, well, great."

I glanced over at her friends. They were cut from the same cloth as Layla—cute, friendly, and lightly flirtatious. I sensed Layla had implied our connection might be more than it actually was. She slipped her hand through my elbow, bumping her hip against mine, and even leaned up to press a kiss on my cheek.

None of which I would have had a problem with, except it was awkward. That, and what she offered wasn't something I wanted anymore. Fuck my life.

They were with me for a three-hour flightseeing trip. By the end of it, my nerves were on edge with Layla's flirting grating on me. I was beyond relieved when I landed back at the small airport in Diamond Creek and the locals scheduled for my next flight were already waiting along with boxes of mail and groceries to deliver.

Skylar's voice came through my headset moments after I landed. "Hey, Grant. We've got some extra groceries. Do you think you have some room?"

I glanced at the list of passengers, then replied, "Sure do."

"All right. I'll have Dan meet you over there."

"Perfect."

Layla smiled up at me, practically batting her eyelashes. She was laying it on thick today. "What are you up to tonight?" she asked.

"It's staff night out at the lodge," I replied.

"Oh, what's that?"

"A work meeting." That wasn't a complete lie, but

it was a misrepresentation. Yes, all the people I worked with would physically be in the same location, but it wasn't required by any stretch.

"Okay. Well, have fun," she said in a singsong tone that was like fingernails on a chalkboard by this point. "You know where to reach me. Hopefully, we'll see you out sometime this week."

"Sure. Take care," I called with a wave as she finally turned to leave.

Chapter Eight

HARLEY

"Harley?" a woman's voice called.

I stood from the chair in the waiting room at the doctor's office. "Right here," I called as I hurried toward the reception desk where she was waiting.

She smiled at me. "Hi, I'm Dr. Quinn's medical assistant, Carla."

"Hi, I'm Harley."

She gestured to a door beside the desk. "Follow me," she said as she held it open.

I followed her down a short hallway into an examination room. I liked Carla. She had an easy, comfortable manner to her. A few minutes later, she'd run through all the basics with me. I'd explained that I already knew what was going on with my heart.

"So, your previous doctor didn't prescribe any medication?" She cocked her head to the side, her gaze curious.

"I wanted to try to manage it without medication," I said, my words halting.

She nodded. "Well, that's definitely an option. How often are you having these episodes?"

I wanted to lie. I really did. "Maybe once a week," I finally said, forcing myself to be truthful.

She simply nodded and typed something. "Dr. Quinn should be with you in a few minutes," she said before departing.

I waited alone in the room with anxiety spinning in my chest. None of my family or friends knew I had been diagnosed with a heart condition, supraventricular tachycardia, or SVT. That was a really long way of saying I had an erratic heartbeat, typically extra heartbeats.

Since I was a little girl, I'd experienced times when it felt like my heart went way too fast. Roughly two years ago, I'd passed out at work. Fortunately, I was alone at my desk where I worked for a tech company on graphics.

After the third time something like that happened, I'd finally gone in to see a doctor. They'd had me wear a heart monitor for two weeks and gently recommended I consider medication. My family would freak right out and worry like crazy if they knew anything about this. I didn't want anybody to know. I hated any sign of weakness. It was beyond frustrating that Grant had come in after I'd fainted the other night.

I still thought I had plausible deniability if he mentioned it to Diego. I would just say I had low blood sugar. I thought that was a good line of bullshit. A few minutes later, there was a light knock on the door.

"Come on in," I called.

The doctor who entered the room was surprisingly handsome with amber hair, eyes to match, and a fit build. He smiled over at me. "Hi, Harley. I'm Dr. Haynes. You can also just call me Quinn." He tapped his fingertips on his name tag, which read Quinn.

"Dr. Quinn, the medicine man," I quipped.

He chuckled at that. "You'll see me in the grocery store, so it's easier to go by first names. Looks like you work out at Walker Adventures."

I nodded. "Yep. My brother is one of the pilots there, Diego Jackson."

"Ah, I know Diego. Small world. I go to Gemma's yoga classes too."

I smiled. "I love her classes."

He sat down on a wheeled chair that had a curved desk with a computer screen mounted on it. He tapped a few keys. "So, it looks like your prior doctor diagnosed you with SVT?" I nodded. "Let's cover the basics," he added.

He checked my heartbeat, my lungs, and so on before returning to his chair. "I appreciate you making sure these records were sent over ahead of time."

"Sure."

"What prompted you to come in?" he asked.

"Uh, I had another episode."

"You're having those about once a week?" he asked.

"Uh-huh."

His eyes were trained on the computer monitor. "It says here you wanted to see if you could manage this without medication." His attention lifted to me.

I took a breath. "Yeah. I'd prefer that."

He nodded before looking back at the computer monitor and then at me. "Based on the monitoring report from before..." He lifted a hand, wiggling it back and forth in the air. "You're on that line."

"What line?"

"The line where I'd like to recommend medication. I'm concerned that these episodes are occurring weekly. You're young, and I want you to be comfortable with medication before we do that. It looks like this last round of monitoring was from two years ago when you were diagnosed."

I braced myself for the lecture. When none came, I let out a sharp sigh.

"You can look up at me. I'm not going to lecture you," he said dryly. "Most people are nervous about going to the doctor and even more so when they have an actual medical issue. SVT is manageable. I want to see what's going on for you now. Are you comfortable wearing a heart monitor again?"

"Of course."

"Good. I'll get you set up with one before you leave."

"You have one here?"

"There are some downsides to being rural, but an upside is when I order things, I keep a small stock so I don't have to send you somewhere else."

"Well, that's handy."

He flashed me a grin. "We'll schedule an appointment in two weeks and discuss your options when we get that report back. Sound like a plan?"

I nodded. "That's it?"

"That's it. I'm curious, though. Your records don't indicate any known family history of cardiac issues."

I shook my head. "I don't know of any."

"Have you ever asked?"

"No." My cheeks felt hot.

"If you feel comfortable asking, these things are good to know. They help us make informed decisions."

"I'll ask," I said quietly.

"You don't have to, but it would definitely be helpful."

He stood, holding his hand out. "Good to meet you," he said as I shook his hand. "Hope to see you around town or maybe at a yoga class."

"Thank you," I called as he departed the room.

Moments later, I walked quickly to the waiting area. The receptionist smiled up at me. "Carla is getting your monitor ready for you."

A woman came through the doorway behind the reception desk. She had auburn hair and a lithe build. She smiled at me. "Hey."

"Hi," I returned.

"This is Lacey, Quinn's wife," the receptionist said.

"You don't have to announce it every time I come out. I was just stopping by to print something. My printer broke," Lacey explained.

The receptionist grinned. "Your printer has been broken for over two months."

Lacey let out a sigh. "I'll get it fixed, I swear." She glanced at me. "You look familiar, but I'm not sure why."

"I moved here just over a year ago. Quinn said he goes to Gemma's yoga classes. I go to her class in town maybe once a week."

"Oh, that's probably where I've seen you," she replied.

"I'm Harley, Harley Jackson. I work out at Walker Adventures and do online stuff for websites, graphic design, that kind of thing."

"Oh, that's awesome. My sister, Marley, does tech stuff too. Oh, hey, your names rhyme," she commented.

I laughed. "I actually know Marley. We've met a few times. She sends us customers, and we do the same in return."

"Well, it's nice to meet you. Wait a sec. Are you Diego's sister?"

I held a thumb up. "Good guess."

The receptionist handed Lacey a sheaf of papers as they finished printing. "There you go."

Lacey disappeared with a smile and a wave. Carla came out front and briefly reviewed how to use the heart monitor. I still wasn't thrilled with this heart situation, but I liked my new doctor. As I began the drive back to Walker Adventures, I tried to think of how to ask anyone in my family about their health history. I had three sisters in Texas and Diego here. They all had opinions. I didn't want anyone to worry.

"Yes!" Cat announced, punching a fist into the air.

Grant leaned back in the cushions as he tossed his cards on the coffee table. "I give up."

"You do?" I couldn't help but laugh.

Cat had persuaded Grant and me to play cards with her. She said she needed to prepare for card nights since they would happen at some point.

"Is this going to be a weekly thing?" Grant asked.

Cat shrugged. "I was thinking once a month. Is that a problem?"

Grant rolled his eyes. "It's more fun when it's just the guys."

"Well, you live with two women now, so deal with it," Cat retorted.

I bit back a laugh. Grant looked up. The second his eyes met mine, heat sizzled through me. I'd been doing a fairly good job, I thought, of avoiding him. I knew it would be weird if I alerted Cat to that avoidance by declining to join them tonight since we lived together. I was relieved when he broke away from my gaze first.

Grabbing my glass of wine, I took a swallow. As a disciplined person, I was determined to get myself over this stupid lust crush. "Lush" was what my friend back in Texas called them.

Three days later

"What the hell?" I demanded as I slammed the door behind me.

Grant was seated at the kitchen table. He was wearing a T-shirt and sweatpants with his feet propped up on another chair.

I thrust my jacket off my shoulders, hanging it up and kicking my shoes off as I dropped my purse onto the table by the door. "What did you tell Diego?" I walked quickly through the living room into the kitchen.

"I told him I came in and was pretty sure you'd fainted. I also told him I told you to see a doctor."

"Grrrr," I muttered. "How could you do that?"

"Harley, I was concerned about you. I didn't realize it was a secret."

"Well, Diego's freaking out."

"Well, maybe if you went to the doctor, nobody would be worried. Did you go see the doctor?"

"Yes," I ground out. I curled my arms around my waist, spinning away and pacing back and forth by the table.

"I'm not sure why you're upset. I bet you'd say something to Cat, or Flynn, or Nora if you found me passed out," Grant pointed out.

He was right, but I wasn't about to let him know

that. I threw my hands up in the air, letting them fall. I stomped back over to him, resting my hands on my hips as I glared at him.

He leaned forward, tossing his phone onto the table, way too calm and relaxed about this.

"So what did the doctor say?"

"Well, it's none of your fucking business, but I am fine. You know medical information is private," I said.

Grant rolled his eyes. "Fine. You don't have to tell me, but if you've got something going on, maybe you could let your family know."

I flung my hands in the air again. Grant leaned back in his chair. "If you don't want people to think this is a big deal, maybe you shouldn't be so mad about it."

"Oh. My. God."

While I normally had to look up at Grant since I was short and he was tall, we were almost eye level with him seated and me standing. I leaned forward, pressing my fingertip into his chest.

Grant's silvery-blue eyes met mine, darkening. I abruptly realized, way too late, that I was *waaa-yyy* too close to him. With my fingertip pressed into his chest, I could feel the heat emanating from him. It traveled up my arm, flames flickering and radiating outward. My belly flipped, and my breath became short.

I tried to tell myself to back away, but I couldn't. I clung to my anger like a lifeline. "You shouldn't have told Diego anything. It's my business."

Grant didn't look away. It felt as if he were meeting the dare I'd flung in his direction and catching the fiery arrow of it. He actually shrugged, narrowing his eyes. "What exactly are you going to do about it?"

I opened my mouth to say something, but then I leaned closer. I didn't know what I wanted. I didn't intend to kiss him, but maybe I was. I still hadn't forgotten our kiss from the other night. I'd told myself for days that I would remember all the reasons kissing Grant Walker was a foolish, stupid idea and never kiss him again.

Foolish or not, my body had its own opinion. Our mouths met, and it felt as if lightning bolts struck between us. I was fighting a war within myself, and it was futile. His hand slid around to cup my nape, drawing me closer.

All rational thought scattered like leaves blown away with a bracing gust of wind. I shimmied onto his lap, straddling him. He was all lean muscle, fluid under my touch, warm and strong and hard in more places than one. I shimmied even closer, savoring the feel of his arousal against me.

I gasped when he snaked an arm around my waist, banding me tight against him. All of this felt so good. My nipples ached where they pressed against his muscled chest.

I broke free from his mouth, sucking in deep lungfuls of air. Our eyes met, and we stared at each other. It was as if we had an entire conversation without words.

This is crazy.

I know. But it feels so good.

I know.

It's stupid.

I know, but I want you too much.

I didn't realize I whispered that last part aloud until he whispered in return, "I know. I do too."

On the heels of another breath, we were kissing again. He drew away too soon. For a split second, I thought he was going to be the sane one. He would tell me we should stop right now and slam the brakes on this madness.

Instead, he nipped at my earlobe, and I shivered in his arms, biting my lip. I tried to hold back a moan, but it slipped out. His lips teased at the sensitive skin just beneath my ear before blazing a trail of hot kisses down my neck. One kiss followed the next with a soft brush of his lips, open and wet. Goose bumps broke out all over my skin, and sensation sizzled down my spine in a fiery shiver.

He muttered something, lifting his head and hooking his hand on the hem of my shirt. In another second, cool air struck my skin as he lifted it up and over my head. I was a practical woman for the most part, except when it came to my underwear. Today, I wore a deep navy silk bra, the cups barely covering my nipples.

Grant's gaze dipped down and then lifted to mine again, the look there dark.

"Fuck, Harley," he whispered.

His knuckles trailed across the tops of my breasts as he lowered his head. His tongue teased just above the silk before he dipped lower, his mouth closing over one of my nipples through the silk. My finger speared his hair, and I cried out sharply.

He lifted his head again. "You're so fucking sexy."

I opened my mouth to argue. He put a finger over my lips. "Don't argue with me."

I fumbled to reach for his shirt, demanding, "Take your shirt off."

"Yes, ma'am," he returned, his lips curling in a sly smile as he reached behind his head.

He yanked his shirt off, and then all of that muscle was pressed against me. His skin was warm to the touch and felt like fire against mine. The contrast of

his hard-muscled chest against my softness was intox-
icating.

Sensations overrode my sanity. It was as if the fuse
box in my brain was flicked off. All reason was over-
ridden by the pure need, want, and fire storming
through my system.

His palm splayed on my lower back and then slid
up my spine, levering me forward as he fit his mouth
to mine in a devouring, claiming kiss. Grant was such
an easygoing guy, always quick with a smile and light-
ness to his laugh. I didn't expect this intensity, this
edge of possessiveness.

Our tongues dueled, and I felt myself tumbling, my
need for control falling to the wayside in the rush of
this tide of desire to simply let myself be claimed by
this man. And claim me, he did. One devouring kiss
after another.

His hands mapped my body, cupping my breasts
and teasing them until I was begging, "Grant, please…"

His low chuckle against my skin sent fire licking
over the surface. My bra fell away, and his lips closed
over a nipple. The hot shock of it released a ragged
cry from me. I rocked my hips over his thick swollen
length nestled at the apex of my thighs. The rough
friction created by our clothes generated this sweet,
piercing pleasure that was spinning and cresting in
little waves. I felt my release teetering, and I wanted it
so bad.

Grant murmured, "Hang on."

He set me back off his lap. I felt bereft and nearly
protested.

He had so much more control than I did. He
unbuttoned my jeans, and his fingers slipped between
my thighs as he shoved them down. I was wet, drip-
ping wet, slippery with arousal. His eyes held mine,

and I couldn't look away as he delved into the very heart of me. With my jeans still half on, the friction was intense. His fingers pumped in and out, the heel of his palm riding over my clit again and again.

I tried to cling to some control, but I couldn't. My orgasm hit me abruptly, those tiny waves of pleasure rolling into a massive, crashing release. I let out a choked cry as I shuddered all over, my knees giving out as he pulled me onto his lap.

The pleasure seemed to go on and on and on, finally slowing with tiny waves lapping through me. I was limp and sated as I sat there curled against him. He slowly withdrew his fingers, and I dragged my eyes open. He was watching me, looking as stunned as I felt, which was a relief.

I nearly came again when he lifted his fingers and licked them, murmuring, "I need to know what you taste like."

He dropped his hand and kissed me again. I tasted the subtle tang of my own arousal against his lips. A moment later, he lifted his head, murmuring, "Cat will be here any minute."

I scrambled off his lap, and we yanked our clothes back on in a rush. I glanced at the clock, realizing she usually did get here around this time because she did baking prep for the following morning. Just then, I heard her footsteps on the stairs.

Chapter Ten

GRANT

"Grant?" Skylar prompted, waving her hand in front of my face.

"Hmm?" I glanced down.

She looked up, her big blue eyes blinking at me. "You with me here, dude?"

"Oh yeah, sorry."

Tucker, one of the other pilots and Skylar's boyfriend, approached. "I have room."

"For what?" I asked.

Skylar glanced at Tucker and then back at me, rolling her eyes. "You are seriously out of it today."

"What are you talking about?"

"I just asked you how much room you had for that pallet." She thumbed over her shoulder toward the pallet in question.

"Oh," I said.

Tucker cast me a sideways glance. "Everything all right?"

"Everything's fine," I muttered.

Everything *was* fine. Except Harley had blown my

mind three nights ago, and I couldn't stop thinking about it. We were both doing a bang-up job of avoiding each other since then, yet I couldn't stop thinking about her. It was so bad. I even tried to hook up with Layla last night, but I couldn't even kiss her. It was crazy. I felt like I'd lost my mind.

Tucker peered into the back of my plane, glancing over at Skylar as he straightened. "Let's put half in his plane and half in mine."

I mentally kicked myself, glancing back and forth between them and offering, "Sounds like a plan. I can't take that whole pallet. What is it anyway?"

"Food," Skylar replied. "Let's get to it."

The three of us quickly loaded up both of our planes. When we were done, Skylar smiled. "Thanks, you guys."

Tucker leaned down to kiss her. "See you tonight."

I waved and climbed into my plane. My day started out with transport and then handling some local flights. Tourists required a little more conversation usually, so that would make my day easier.

Midmorning, I landed in Seldovia, where my friend Tom was waiting. He smiled at me, waggling his eyebrows. "What have you got today? The store is totally out of milk, so I hope you have some."

"I don't know what's in those crates, but probably some milk. Tucker will be here in a bit with more," I replied.

He grinned. "I'm sure there is."

He helped me unload, offering, "Make this flight back quick. I'm gonna be late for my doctor's appointment."

"Am I late?" I asked.

"No. I'm late." He chuckled. "I was supposed to

take the flight with Nora earlier, but, well, I overslept."

I laughed as I opened the passenger door. "Hop in the front, man. Nobody else is with me for this one."

"Nice. Can we chat?"

"Of course." Tom was a regular customer. Most of the locals were regulars.

That was one of the things I loved about my job. I enjoyed flying and got to fly over the breathtaking landscape of Alaska every day. We completed a variety of tasks, such as taking tourists out for sightseeing and handling transport for goods and locals. It was a one-of-a-kind job, and I wouldn't trade it for the world.

Once we were up in the air, we began chatting on the private channel on the headset, discussing the weather, business, and the like. Tom commented that he needed to pick up a gift for his anniversary.

"Oh, yeah?"

"Yeah, this is wife number four, but she was also my first wife. So really, she's wife number one," he offered with a chuckle. I couldn't help but laugh. "Hey, we figured it out in time," he added.

"What are you going to get her?"

"I don't know. I'm really shitty at getting gifts. I am good at remembering that I need to get them, though."

"Well, what does she like?" I asked.

"That's the thing. She's got everything. She always says I shouldn't worry about it."

"Well, maybe you should do something for her."

"What do you mean do something for her?"

"I don't know. There's that new spa in Diamond Creek."

"Ooh, I could get her a gift certificate. She could get a massage and stuff?"

"Yes, exactly. They're in the place right beside Gemma's yoga studio."

I happened to know he occasionally went to Gemma's yoga classes when he was over in Diamond Creek.

"I love this idea. You are good. If you ever settle down, you'll be good at gifts."

I shrugged. "This was one idea. How long have you been married?"

"Well, if I count our first few years and now..." He quickly did the math on his fingers. "Twenty years."

"How old are you?" I asked.

He waggled his eyebrows. "Only sixty-four. I figure we can hit at least our fortieth anniversary. I'm gonna make it to one hundred. I have goals." I chuckled. "What about you? Are you serious with anybody?"

I shook my head. "Nah."

"All your friends are getting married. Don't you think it's your turn?"

I slid him a look. "Are you serious, dude?"

"Well, no, but yeah," he returned.

I burst out laughing. "Which one is it?"

He shrugged. "I don't know. How old are you?"

"Thirty."

"It's about time you stop being stupid. That's when I started to figure shit out."

Of course, my mind went straight to Harley because, well, she'd come all over my fingers the other night. It had been the hottest thing I'd ever experienced—her in my arms climaxing. Just now, even when I shouldn't be, I felt a stirring down there. That was how bad I had it for her.

I surprised myself with my question. "How did you know?"

"Know what?"

"When it was the right person?"

"I was stupid when I was young," he announced in his typically direct manner. "I actually knew with my first wife, but I was just not the brightest guy then. We were young when we first got together. I won't say I didn't love my second and third wives, but it wasn't quite the same. With us, we just clicked. But it doesn't mean it's easy. It really isn't easy with her. She's the one who challenges me the most. The simple part is the trust."

"What do you mean by that?"

"Just knowing that on a base level when shit gets hard, you're going to be there for each other and have each other's backs. Does that make any sense? We still argue. Hell, when we fight, it's loud. She's kind of got a temper, and so do I. That's how we ended up divorced when we were younger. We've mellowed now that we're older. Now, when we get going, we end up laughing." He rolled his eyes. "I don't think I'm explaining this well, but she's solid for me."

I nodded slowly. "I think I know what you mean."

"Why? Got somebody in mind?" he teased.

I cast him a glare. "No," I lied. "Just wondering. I mean, like you pointed out, my whole family's freaking falling in love now except for Cat."

"Well, she's way too young," he offered. "She gonna fly planes too?"

"She used to say she wanted to, but she loves cooking at the lodge," I stated.

"Then she should follow her passion for now. She can always change her mind."

A short while later, we landed and climbed out of the plane. Just as he was about to amble off, Tom glanced back. "I think you do have somebody in mind. Don't be stupid like me."

"What do you mean?"

"Get it right the first time." He winked before waving and walking away.

Chapter Eleven

GRANT

I took a bite of my burger, closing my eyes before opening them again. "Their burgers are fucking good."

"I know," Flynn replied.

I took a swallow of my beer, glancing around the table. Every few weeks, the guys tried to get together. Tonight, it was actually all of us—Flynn, Diego, Tucker, Gabriel, Elias, and myself. We'd met up at Glacier Brewery, which had excellent food to go along with the beer.

"Schedule's busy these days," Diego commented between bites of his burger.

Flynn nodded. "I know. For now, we're just going to roll with it. I'm not up for buying another plane or hiring another pilot right now."

"I get it, man. It's a lot to manage," Elias replied.

Our conversation meandered along, talking about work and our respective lives. Diego happened to be seated beside me. Flynn was chatting with Gabriel about something on one of the planes, and Diego commented to me, "Thanks for letting me know about Harley, by the way. She upset with you about it?"

"Oh, yeah," I replied with a chuckle. I ignored the jolt of heat that went through me at any mention of Harley.

Diego's sister had definitely been upset with me. Then I'd lost my damn mind and kissed her again. That ended with her coming all over my fingers. I was so fucked.

I forced my mind to the moment. "She said she went to the doctor."

"Yeah?" he prompted.

"She said it turned out to be no big deal. Just a low blood sugar thing."

"Hope she's telling the truth," he commented.

"You don't think she is?"

Diego shrugged. "It's Harley, and she doesn't like to make a big deal out of fucking anything."

"Mmm," I offered. The last thing I wanted was to spend more time talking about Harley. It was bad enough to have her parked smack dab in the middle of my thoughts most of the time.

Later that night as I lay in bed, I was attuned to any tiny sound coming from her bedroom. This was day four of managing to avoid her at the house. Yet she was here, just on the other side of the wall between our rooms.

Her door had been firmly closed when I'd gotten home. My mind replayed Diego's last comment about Harley. I hoped it was nothing, and that she wasn't covering up something more serious. My mother had passed away from an undiagnosed heart defect when I was in college. Her death still weighed on me. She'd had problems periodically but hadn't told us the whole story. I remembered being worried, but she'd assured me she was fine and insisted I go to college.

It was midsemester one year when I got the emergency call. The doctor had told us her prognosis wouldn't have been good long-term because of the complications. But still, I kept thinking if I hadn't been off at college, somehow, she would've been okay. I'd raced home to take care of Nora and Cat while I tried to hold our family together until Flynn could get there for all of us.

After Flynn came home, things started to feel less overwhelming. But even now, I carried the weight of it. Old twinges of guilt burned. I thought I should have known. Logically, I knew better, but it didn't really matter.

While I understood Harley was angry with me for mentioning it to Diego, she didn't understand where I was coming from. My mind spun. Moments from the other night kept going off like little flashbulbs in my memories. Every recollection triggered a visceral response as my body reacted with lingering jolts of electricity.

Diego would fucking kill me if he knew I'd even thought about his sister that way, much less had done anything about it. I thought maybe I could get over my attraction to Harley if she wasn't fucking living here.

———

I glanced over at Tucker, who was walking through the garage door to one of our plane hangars. "Hey!" I called as he approached.

"Hey, want to grab some dinner at Sally's?" he asked.

"You're not doing anything with Skylar?"

Tucker grinned as he shook his head. "She's working late tonight. She and Ludie are going over the monthly accounting. She stresses out about that. They're all set up with takeout."

"I'm your second choice then," I replied wryly.

Tucker reached me, cuffing me lightly on the shoulder. "No, you're my friend, and I like hanging out."

"You can be honest. I know it's just because she's busy," I teased.

He rolled his eyes. "Don't I show up when we all meet at the brewery?"

"You do."

"Let's go to Sally's. I'll be your wingman, and I'll bow out with perfect timing," he offered, waggling his brows.

"I don't need a wingman, dude."

"Don't you, though?" he teased.

"No," I countered, shrugging off the subtle irritation I felt.

Of late, I'd gotten annoyed at how I was often teased as if I was some kind of player. I wasn't. I just wasn't interested in anything serious.

"Let me close up here."

I quickly leaned into the front of the plane, snagging my backpack where it sat on the floor just behind the seat.

Tucker crossed the garage, calling, "You need anything from the office, or can I turn the light out?"

"Lights out," I called in return.

A moment later, we closed the garage bay door and walked out the side entrance together.

Tucker paused, his gaze arcing from the plane hangars to the marshy field and the mountains beyond. "Damn. I've been here for over five years now, and I still haven't gotten used to these long days."

I shrugged. "It's all I've ever known. When I was a

teenager, I stayed up so late, always just doing my own thing."

"It helps to have the blackout shades. When I first moved here, I didn't see the point. I'm smarter now," he commented.

"When I was a kid, we couldn't afford those, so we put tinfoil on the windows."

Tucker chuckled. We followed each other over to Sally's because Tucker claimed he would leave sooner than I did. I would prove him wrong. I was in a new phase of responsibility and didn't feel the need to stay out late and party. I told myself this had nothing to do with Harley. Not a thing.

A short while later, we were seated at a booth. Sally's was an old barn renovated into a restaurant and bar. The kitchen was in the center with the restaurant on one side with booths and tables, and the other side had smaller tables and a stage for music. The old hayloft had been renovated into loft seating. The place had a relaxed, casual feel with wide-plank hardwood flooring worn after years of feet crossing over them. It was a favorite local hangout with organized card nights, karaoke nights, open mic, and the like. It also had good pub fare, nothing fancy, and always consistent.

Tucker lifted his pint of beer, clinking his glass against mine. "To one beer tonight."

I chuckled. "Yeah, we're both driving. So how are things with Skylar?"

He finished his swallow of beer, his lips twitching with a smile. "Good, really good."

"Good," I returned. "You deserve it."

"Yeah? I never understood why people say things like that."

"What do you mean?"

"Well, don't you think everybody deserves something good in life? I don't think I'm any more special than anybody else," he offered.

I shrugged. "Okay, fair enough. But you had someone you loved, and she died, so it feels like you should catch a lucky break. How about letting yourself just enjoy this?"

He chuckled. "Old habits die hard and all that."

"I get it."

His gaze sobered. "I suppose you do. Both of your parents died when you were pretty young."

I took a swallow of my beer, nodding in agreement. "Yeah. Our dad wasn't exactly around much. I miss him, but he was pretty inconsistent. My mom, though. That was a hit." I lightly thumped my fist over my heart.

"How old were you when it happened?"

"I was in college. We knew she had some heart issues, but we didn't know the extent. She collapsed, and they couldn't restart her heart." I swallowed, my throat feeling tight for a minute.

Grief sometimes felt like little arrows randomly striking and stinging deeply. "She was everything for all of us."

"It hurts to lose someone like that."

"It does. I still miss her."

"Flynn was with us. I remember he got that call, and then he was making arrangements to go home."

"I was up in Anchorage. I drove home that night, of course, as soon as I heard. Nora was sixteen, and Cat wasn't even a teenager yet. They were trying to figure out if there should be a temporary guardianship since I was only in college. Thank God, they got Flynn on the phone. He promised he was making arrangements to get home. Without Flynn, I don't know what we would have done. There's no way I could have pulled off what he did with the family business. My mom had done her best, but it was slow going. It was nothing like what we have now, in large part thanks to all of you coming out to fly."

Tucker held my gaze, nodding slowly. "Well, we all love to fly. Flynn would have made it work without us, though."

"Maybe. But I like it this way. It feels like we're all a family."

"Damn straight, we are," he said firmly.

The server arrived to take our food order. After we ordered, Layla stopped by, slipping into the booth beside me.

"Hey." She nudged me playfully with her shoulder.

I grinned down at her. She smiled over at Tucker, asking politely about Skylar and so on. She made herself comfortable.

A while later, Tucker departed with a wink and a smile, clapping me on the shoulder. "See you tomorrow. If I don't see you at work, I'll be out at the lodge for yoga."

"All right. Have a good one," I replied.

Then it was Layla and me. "How have you been? I haven't seen you out much," she commented.

"Just been busy."

I decided then and there I needed to distract myself from Harley and that sizzling electric encounter the other night. I slid my arm around Layla's shoulders. "Where are you headed?"

"Home," she answered, her blue eyes blinking when she smiled up at me.

All of this should have gotten my engine revving. Instead, I just wasn't feeling it. I told myself we would go out to the parking lot and I would kiss her to get me started.

Wrong. I couldn't even bring myself to kiss her.

"Something wrong, Grant?" she asked when we were standing by her car.

"Nah. Good to see you."

She leaned up, pressing a kiss on my cheek and catching my hand to reel me closer. I shook my head. "Not tonight."

I drove home with Harley on my mind.

Chapter Twelve

HARLEY

Several days later, I was back at the doctor's office, and Quinn was waiting patiently. I stared down at my hands before lifting my eyes to his again. He was a little too handsome to be a doctor, but I liked him. He had this comfortable, relaxed manner to him.

"I don't want to take medication," I finally said.

He took a breath, nodding in acknowledgment before replying, "I understand that, but I think it would help. I'm concerned if you don't—"

I shook my head, anger rising swiftly inside. "Why? It's just an irregular heartbeat," I argued.

"It's not quite that simple. It's erratic, and it affects the oxygen flow in your system. That's what's causing the fainting episodes. Can you help me understand what you're concerned about, and why you're so opposed to medication?"

My irritation felt prickly. I wanted to shake the feeling away. I didn't want to explain. That meant admitting I didn't like having weakness of any kind. "I've been doing fine without it," I finally said, my voice sounding a little sharper than I intended.

"Okay. Look, let's schedule a follow-up. I'd like you to think about it. I'm going to give you some information that explains what's happening and how the medication will help."

"Okay. Aren't you supposed to listen to what I want?" I pressed.

Quinn was entirely unruffled by my snappiness. "I *am* listening, but as your doctor, it's my responsibility to be honest with you about what I recommend and what's best for your health. I do respect if you choose not to take the medication. Maybe when you're more comfortable with me, you can explain why. In the meantime, let's schedule a follow-up. You can review the information and think about the medication."

I kept my temper in check. It wasn't his fault. This was actually the same thing my other doctor had told me.

"This will significantly decrease your likelihood of having these episodes."

"What episodes?" I asked as if I didn't know.

"The fainting, the breathlessness, and temporary weakness."

I rolled my eyes. "Fine. I'll think about it."

He stood and was opening the door when I said, "Dr. Haynes." He turned back. "I'm not annoyed with you. I'm annoyed with the situation."

"You can be annoyed with me, but I appreciate the clarification."

Between that and having to have a conversation with Diego and our sisters about this, I was feeling, well, snippy about it. Apparently, there was a family history of heart issues. I'd had to listen to a little lecture from my oldest sister. My mom's sister had the same thing I did.

I'd lied to all of them and told them it was mild

and no medication had been recommended. I didn't like to lie, but I also didn't want to deal with my family's overbearing attitude since I was the youngest of five siblings with bossy sisters and an overprotective older brother. For the first time since it had happened, my mind flung itself in the direction of Grant.

It was a relief to think about him later that night even though all of that mess was an inconvenient and consuming distraction. He was a better option than worrying about the stupid heart thing.

It still chafed me that he had told Diego. Like I needed another overprotective guy in my life. That evening, Cat wasn't at the staff house. She was in Anchorage with a friend for the whole weekend. Which meant it was just Grant and me.

That didn't have to mean anything, or so I told myself. It wasn't like he was here every night anyway or that our schedules aligned. I often hung out at the lodge with Daphne and Nora. Or I holed up in my room to read and work late on projects. With my job primarily online, my bed could be my desk. I didn't have to interact with Grant.

Except tonight I wanted to. I wanted a distraction. Badly.

When I stopped by the lodge, Daphne was busy with guests. With Cat up in Anchorage, she was busier than usual. I offered to help. I basically just followed her instructions in the kitchen, stirring this, cleaning that, putting things on the table for the guests, and playing tourist guide for those with questions about the area and what to do.

I kept wondering if Grant would make an appearance. Staff usually swung by and grabbed something for dinner unless they were otherwise occupied. The

moment he showed up, I felt a fiery prickle of awareness race down my spine.

I forced myself to finish what I was doing, putting
the latest round of dishes through the industrial-sized
dishwasher in the back. I turned to see him standing
at the counter laughing at something Flynn said. He
reached for one of the stuffed savory rolls Daphne had
made for appetizers. She had left extras out for the
staff.

Flynn turned his attention to Daphne, leaning over
and asking her a question. As Grant chewed, his eyes
arced around the kitchen before they landed on where
I stood in the back by the dishwasher, drying my
hands with a towel.

Our gazes collided. I felt caught in a beam, and my
belly shimmied, sending tingles through my system. I
paid close attention to what I was doing. I finished
drying my hands on the towel and looked away, tossing
it in the laundry basket under the sink.

I told myself to play it cool. Daphne turned when I
stopped beside where she was putting away the pots
and pans.

"Thank you for your help," she said with a smile.
"With Cat gone, there's extra for me to do."

"Always glad to help. You want me to help over the
weekend?"

"Well, you don't have to."

"I'm offering," I replied with a smile.

"I'd love it. Thank you." She leaned over, curling an
arm around my shoulders and squeezing me before
stepping away.

"Are we done?" I asked.

"Everything's put away," she said.

"Daphne, these are amazing," Grant commented as
he finished another savory roll. "What's in them?"

"Swiss cheese with caramelized onions and roast beef."

"The pastry is seriously good," he replied.

"Well, there's a lot of butter in it," Daphne replied with a grin. "You can take the rest with you if you'd like."

"Hey, wait a sec," Flynn interjected, his eyes widening.

Daphne rolled her eyes. "I already put some in our apartment."

"Oh, thank God." Flynn sighed.

Grant smiled at them. "Dude, you are so spoiled. You know she'd stay up and make you extra if you wanted."

"I know, but I wouldn't ask her." Flynn scoffed.

Daphne shrugged. "I wouldn't mind. I love to bake. Here." She crossed over to another counter and returned with a piece of foil to neatly wrap the remaining rolls.

"There's my breakfast tomorrow," Grant said. "Thank you."

"Anytime."

"Good night," Flynn said, rounding the counter and reaching for Daphne's hand.

They disappeared through the door to the hallway that led to their apartment, leaving Grant and me alone in the kitchen. I glanced up at Grant. The space suddenly felt crowded, and it wasn't small by any stretch. Daphne had already turned out the lights in the dining room area, leaving just the dim lights on in the kitchen.

I glanced toward the windows, looking for any distraction. The moon rose above the mountains, casting a pearly glow over the landscape and illuminating a cluster of cottonwood trees nearby.

The sound of my swallow was audible as I turned back. Grant was simply standing there with his hand resting on the edge of the counter. I sucked in a quick breath, and even that seemed loud. My heart was pounding, the rush of blood echoing in my ears with every beat.

"Well..." I heard myself whispering, my voice coming out raspy.

Grant's gaze was locked with mine.

"Well, what?" he pressed, his low voice sending my belly into spinning flips.

I swallowed again, making a quick and perhaps disastrous decision. This chemistry between us wasn't going anywhere. After the other night and knowing the magic he wrought with his touch, I couldn't stop thinking about him.

The hum of attraction between us snapped and crackled every time we were near each other. I desperately wanted a distraction, anything to stop thinking about my health worries. I knew my heart wouldn't get involved with Grant. Definitely not.

The air around us felt charged. I cleared my throat.

Oh, for fuck's sake. I was annoyed with myself. I wasn't a nervous woman, not usually. I took two strides, closing the distance between us, and lifted a hand. He arched a brow, and his lips twitched at the corners.

"What?" I asked, grabbing onto my prickly response to him like it was a lifeline.

"I was just wondering if you were about to point at me again."

My forefinger literally itched. "No, and why would you say that?" I retorted.

"Because you do it all the time, Harley. Not just to me."

I was already simmering with the heat of my raw lust for him. I got even hotter, my anger stirring the cauldron of desire. "No, I don't."

"Should I ask your brother, or maybe everybody else who knows you?" he countered dryly.

I rolled my eyes. "Whatever. So what if I do?"

He shrugged. "You were about to say something. What did you want?"

One more step and I was right in front of him with mere inches separating us. Grant was all coiled strength and heat and energy. And I wanted him.

I curled my fist around his shirt, tugging him down and murmuring, "This," right before our mouths collided.

Our kiss exploded instantly with our tongues practically at war. Grant shifted closer, his palm landing between my shoulder blades and sliding down my back. His touch was a burning path of heat.

I let out a gasp when his palm curved over my bottom, pressing me tight against his arousal. We broke apart.

I knew my eyes were wide with a combination of shock and need.

"This is stupid," he said flatly.

"No, it's not," I insisted even though a big part of me knew he had a point.

"No?" His gravelly voice sent shivers through me.

"It doesn't have to be anything but this."

"This kiss?" he pressed.

I knew he was daring me to clarify, daring me to take it further.

"Just us, friends with benefits. Nothing more than that." Recklessness and need drove me.

"That's a recipe for complications," he pointed out.

If I was in the mood for logic, I would've agreed

with him. "No, it's not. You don't want a relationship, and neither do I. We've been busy avoiding each other. This way, we don't have to do that. This will scratch the itch, and it'll go away."

I mentally congratulated myself on that twisted logic.

He studied me quietly for several beats. "You think it'll go away?" His tone was laced with doubt.

I nodded, waiting with my pulse thrumming at an all-out gallop and flickers of heat lighting little fires everywhere inside me.

He finally nodded before dipping his head again and claiming my mouth. He took complete control of our kiss.

He held me fast against him. I could feel the brand of his arousal pressed at the apex of my thighs. I was wet and restless, shifting my thighs to relieve the ache and feeling the slick moisture already drenching my panties.

The sound of the front door opening and closing reached us. We broke apart quickly, practically leaping away from each other.

"It's just a guest," I whispered between ragged breaths.

"Yeah, and they can walk in here. Come on." Grant grabbed my hand.

We heard the sound of footsteps coming in the direction of the kitchen just as he tugged me through the doorway into the back hallway. He closed the door quickly, catching it at the last second before it slammed. I stopped, needing to catch my breath. I rested against the wall, my shoulder blades pressed into it as I stood there for a moment.

Grant turned to face me, one palm resting against the wall and the other palming my cheek as he took my mouth in another breath-stealing kiss. I was tingling all over, my breath ragged and my heart pounding wildly.

When he lifted his head, I whispered, "No fair. I was trying to catch my breath. That made it worse."

His eyes were dark with a sly gleam. After a moment, he replied, "This isn't fair."

He reached for one of my hands, placing it over the hard ridge of his arousal. His cock was swollen and hot under my touch. Heat and electricity shot through me as we stared at each other.

He dropped my hand, curling his around mine and leading me outside. We stumbled through the trees, bursting through the door to the staff house moments later.

Grant's mouth and hands were on me the second he kicked the door shut

Chapter Thirteen

GRANT

My hands were pressed against the door as I kissed Harley. She gasped into my mouth. Her tongue twined with mine. I breathed her in, finally breaking free to gulp in desperately needed air.

We stared at each other. I knew this was stupid. It was reckless, and I would regret it. But my need for her was so fierce it trampled over everything else. The only sensible thing to do was to kiss her again. Or that was what my body thought. So I did.

I pulled her away from the door, our lips and teeth clashing. I didn't even think I could manage to get upstairs. We yanked on each other's clothes. When her hand slipped into my boxers, her palm curling around my cock, it pulsed under her touch.

I let out a ragged growl into her mouth, lifting my head and sucking in air. Somewhere along the way, I'd unbuttoned her shirt. Her bra was hanging open with her breasts free. I dipped my head, needing to taste her. I closed my mouth over a nipple and savored her sharp cry.

I spun her around, saying, "Come here."

I shoved her jeans down around her hips. She kicked her shoes off and shimmied out of her jeans.

"Right here," I demanded.

My own jeans were around my ankles with my cock jutting out. She straddled me on the stairs, her eyes meeting mine.

"Fuck, I need a condom," I bit out.

"I'm on the pill," she whispered.

We stared at each other quietly. "Are you sure?"

She nodded.

"I haven't been with anyone for months. And I always use condoms. I can't fucking get you out of my mind," I explained.

"Please," she said.

"Are you sure?" I repeated

In answer, she shimmied closer and slid over the back of my cock. The slide of her slippery folds elicited a groan.

"Oh, sweetheart," I murmured, so out of it I didn't even give myself a mental side-eye for that endearment.

She rose, her eyes on mine. Her lashes started to close before I whispered, "Look at me."

I didn't know why I needed to see her, but I did. I notched myself at her entrance. She rose, the tight peaks of her nipples brushing against my chest. She slid down slowly, bringing me into the slick clench of her core. She bit her lip, her eyes darkening and her mouth opening slightly when she finally seated herself.

It took every ounce of my restraint to keep from coming instantly. We stared at each other, and I hoped the stunned look in her eyes was as intense as I felt. This feeling of being buried deep inside her as she rippled around me felt exactly right. I was precisely where I was supposed to be.

She held still before rocking her hips restlessly. My restraint snapped. My palm slid up her spine as I brought her mouth to mine and began rocking into her. She rose up and sank down, and I thrust to meet every motion. My fingertips pressed into the soft give of her skin as I held her tight to me.

Each thrust was deeper than the last, and I felt her start to shudder around me. Her head fell back as she came with a sharp cry. The sound of her voice calling my name drew my release from me. I came in a ragged burst as she trembled against me. We stared at each other in shock.

Chapter Fourteen

HARLEY

My heartbeat started to slow, and I tried to catch my breath as Grant's gaze held mine. Sensations were still pinging through my body, residual aftershocks of the single most intense climax I'd ever experienced. Here on the stairs. With Grant.

Oh. My. God. This was just supposed to be sex. Except as I sat there with him still buried deep inside me, it felt like something more. As if my heart was almost leaning toward him. There was a subtle tug of a cord between us, an invisible cord I hadn't even known was there.

I scrambled inside, trying to catch my footing emotionally. The only reprieve I felt was that he looked as stunned as I did.

Somehow, we untangled ourselves. The awkward part wasn't that it felt awkward. It was that it *didn't* feel awkward. After I had my shirt buttoned and my jeans on, I glanced over to see him buttoning his jeans.

Our eyes met, and his lips twitched at the corners in a grin I knew well. I'd seen it so many times in the year or so that I'd been staying here.

He fastened the last button and then lifted a hand, lightly cupping my cheek. His thumb trailed along the edge of my jaw, and my pulse raced.

"What?" I asked breathlessly. I'd discovered Grant had the unique ability to steal my breath.

He stepped closer again, dipping his head and giving me a lingering kiss. When he straightened, he asked, "Popcorn and TV?"

That was how I found myself doing what we would usually do, except Cat wasn't there. The only thing missing was Grant and Cat arguing about the shows, which I secretly believed they did just because they thought it was fun. Both of them were too good-natured to really care.

It turned into a normal night. I kept checking myself, doing internal scans. My body felt great, totally relaxed and sated. A mind-blowing orgasm would do that.

The twinges of panic I experienced came solely from the fact that I felt too comfortable with him. It wasn't supposed to feel this comfortable. We should've felt a little awkward.

Almost as if I wanted to force the issue when one show ended and Grant lifted the remote, I said, "We should establish some ground rules."

His hand was suspended in the air for a moment before he lowered it to rest the remote on his thigh. He turned to face me. See, that was the thing with Grant. When he directed his attention on you, it felt like you were the center of his universe. My belly swooped, and I was tingling all over again, almost as if the aftershocks of that earth-shattering climax were still rippling.

"Ground rules?" he prompted.

"Yeah. Cat's not here this weekend. But, news

flash, your little sister lives with us."

Grant chuckled, and my belly swooped again. "She does," he agreed with a firm nod.

A familiar annoyance prickled through me, and I tried to think of what to say.

"So this wasn't a one-time thing?" he asked.

I abruptly felt vulnerable as if I'd stumbled and fallen. That feeling when you're walking along and don't realize there's a step down.

He reached over, sliding his hand just below the base of my neck between my shoulders. I could feel the calloused surface of his fingertips as he squeezed gently. "I don't want it to be a one-time thing."

I barely caught my sigh of relief and met his gaze. "So if Cat's around, nothing can happen on the stairs, or in the kitchen, or in the living room, or in any of the shared spaces."

Grant nodded. "Okay."

Of course, he would agree easily. Jesus, I couldn't even argue with this guy.

"So exactly how is this supposed to happen?" he asked. "We share a bedroom wall, and she doesn't."

"Only after she goes to bed," I said. "Plus, there's usually one or two nights a week that she's not here."

Cat was enjoying her newfound freedom as an official eighteen-year-old. She was responsible but occasionally spent the night with friends and probably a boyfriend she didn't tell anyone about because she had two brothers who might freak out.

I continued, "When she's here, only after she goes to bed, and we *have* to be quiet."

"You're not very quiet," he pointed out, his lips curling in a sly grin.

"You're not either," I retorted.

Then I giggled. I did *not* giggle. That wasn't a thing I did. Except, apparently, I did with Grant.

He pulled me onto his lap, and then we were kissing. We forgot about the TV. Grant slept with me in my bed that night. I couldn't even pretend I didn't love it. I loved that he was cuddly, which I didn't expect. He held me close in his muscled arms, and I woke during the night to his lips pressing a kiss on the side of my neck.

"Grant?" I whispered in the darkness.

"Right here, sweetheart."

Oh. My. God.

When he called me sweetheart, my heart practically swooned.

I didn't giggle, and I didn't swoon. I never had. In fact, Joe, my most recent boyfriend who screwed around on me with my roommate, had said it got a little old with me being all independent. He said I wasn't impressed enough with anything. I kind of thought he meant I wasn't prone to swooning.

I turned over in Grant's arms and straddled him, rolling him onto his back. After that, it was a straight-up tie between that climax and the one earlier on the stairs.

Grant had this little magic trick where, on the one hand, he let me take over and sort of call the shots, but on the other, he was in control the entire time. He played me like an instrument made for him. Another thing I didn't believe in all that made-for anybody bullshit.

So I told myself it was just sex. He was just my roommate and my friend. I was one lucky girl because I got all that and awesome orgasms. I didn't need to worry about the rest.

Chapter Fifteen

GRANT

Thank fuck, my next day was busy even though it was a weekend. We didn't take a single day off in the summer. Not when it came to scheduling flights. We got a last-minute call to cover an overnight trip to Katmai National Forest.

My morning started at seven and didn't end until my last flight touched down. I was grateful for being busy because I needed something to focus on. Even with that, I was half out of it. Holy hell, Harley had blown my fucking mind the night before.

Hot didn't even come close to our time together. Inferno maybe. I was fucked six ways to Sunday. I knew I had a problem on my hands. Like an idiot, I'd thought if I just got her out of my system, that was all I had to do. I'd been crushing on her for over a year. I didn't even know how I was going to look her older brother in the eye.

I felt like I'd broken a few rules. I also knew there was no way I would give Harley up, not yet. I would just deal with the complications.

We would follow her rules because I didn't want

my little sister all up in my business either. I happened to know Cat had a habit of sleeping with earplugs. The reason for it was depressing. Aside from our dad bouncing in and out of our lives, when he was around, he drank and fought a lot with our mom. We'd all dealt with it in our own way. Nora had given Cat a pair of earplugs because Cat would wake up in the night and crawl into Nora's bed when she was scared from his shouting.

I gave myself a mental shake. I didn't need to dwell on things I couldn't ever change.

I would enjoy watching Harley try to stay quiet.

All that weekend, Cat was gone. We used every minute of it to the fullest. I might have been busy during the day, as was Harley. But those two more nights we had? We were both exhausted by the time Monday morning rolled around.

Monday evening, I came back to the staff house a little later than usual. In all honesty, it was because I wanted to make sure Cat and Harley were there. I didn't know if I could keep my hands to myself if I had the chance.

When I walked in through the door, Cat and Harley were on the sectional. Cat was on one side, and Harley was tucked in the corner with her laptop. The scene felt normal. I told myself I could do this without fighting a raging hard-on all night.

"Hey, hey," I called.

Cat leaned her head back, rolling it to the side as she smiled. "Hey!"

"How was your weekend?" I asked as I hung up my

jacket and kicked my shoes into the disorganized shoe tray by the door.

"It was good. Had some good food, hung out with my friend, and did some shopping," Cat replied.

"Get anything good?"

Cat rolled her eyes as I plunked down on the couch across from her. That meant I was actually closer to Harley, but I told myself she had nothing to do with why I sat there. I was talking to Cat so I wanted to face her.

"I wasn't shopping for me. I never shop for myself. I was getting stuff for the lodge—food, supplies for the kitchen, and some part that I had to pick up for Flynn," Cat explained.

"That's usually what I do in Anchorage. How was your day?" I asked as I looked toward Harley.

She tapped something on her keyboard before looking up. I swear to God, the second our gazes collided, bolts of electricity sizzled in the air between us.

"Good," she said. Her tone was casual and relaxed, although I didn't miss the subtle flush cresting on her cheeks. "I worked on the resort website and did some transcription stuff."

"You still do that?" Cat asked.

Harley shrugged. "Here and there. I know this might sound weird, but I actually find it relaxing."

"You do?" Cat and I asked in unison.

Harley grinned as she smiled at us. "I doubt you two would understand since you're both outdoorsy Alaskan types. I kind of get into a zone. I just listen to the recording and type everything out. It's oddly soothing."

"It's medical transcription, right?" Cat prompted.

"Yep. It's doctors transcribing their notes and so

on. I don't do it much. Too much and I get tired of typing."

"But how fast do you type?" I asked.

"Over a hundred words a minute, easy."

Cat's mouth fell open as I gaped. Harley grinned. "I'm sure you too can both shoot and hunt game and fly planes, but I can type."

"I don't fly yet," Cat corrected.

"I know, but I know if you decide to do it, you totally can."

"You could too," Cat insisted.

Harley shrugged. "Maybe so, but I prefer to be a passenger. That responsibility seems a little stressful for me."

"You know, everything comes with some risk," I pointed out. "Statistically speaking, it's less risky than riding in a car."

"Yeah, but that's not how it feels," Harley replied.

"Point one to Harley," Cat teased.

I forced myself to look away. Cat asked me what I wanted to watch, and I shrugged. "I don't care."

"Really?" she pressed.

"Really."

She switched to *Parks and Rec*, one of her favorite comfort shows. "When are we doing card night?" she asked Harley once the show was on. "Soon, right?"

Harley shrugged. "Whenever you want."

"So what's the deal? Am I supposed to be there for it or not?" I asked.

"We're gonna start with just girls because you guys did guys for a long time," Cat said tartly.

"What if the guys want to have a card night?" I countered.

"Well, since you're the only guy who lives here now,

you're outnumbered by the women," Cat said pointedly.

I rolled my eyes. "Fine. We'll do guys' night up at the lodge."

"Sounds like a plan, but Daphne is bringing food over here," Cat returned.

"You know she'll leave some for us."

Cat rolled her eyes and then nodded. "Of course, she will. She's generous like that."

"You would too," Harley interjected.

Cat grinned. "I would."

"Because you're generous like that," Harley repeated.

Except for the fact that I was having trouble with that whole raging hard-on issue, the night was fairly normal. I was pretty positive Cat didn't pick up on anything. Harley went up to bed before we did, which also wasn't unusual. It wasn't set in stone, but she tended to go to bed sooner. Cat was young and still didn't think she needed to sleep. She would scroll on her phone and watch a show in the background for hours most nights.

I went into the kitchen for a glass of water. When I returned to the living room, Cat said, "Your crush is showing."

"Uh, excuse me?" I sat down across from her again.

"Your crush on Harley. It's not a secret, you know."

"Cat," I warned through gritted teeth.

"What?" Her brows hitched up.

"I do *not* have a crush on Harley."

She sighed. "Yeah, you do. It's like when Flynn had his thing for Daphne."

"It is *not* like that," I ground out.

I really didn't think it was like that. Flynn had been head over heels with Daphne pretty much from the day she showed up here. It just took him a while to figure it out.

Cat shrugged. "Suit yourself. I think she kind of likes you too."

"What?" Unfortunately, I didn't catch myself fast enough on that.

Cat burst out laughing. "See, you want to know, don't you?"

I sighed. "Whatever."

"You two have it bad for each other, but you do that thing."

"What thing?"

"Playing it cool. Although she's way worse than you about it."

I knew Cat had a point. I just didn't know Harley had been playing it cool about me. I wasn't about to ask any further questions. I simply said, "Well, I don't know about me, but you're right about Harley. She plays it cool about everything. I'll tell you what. If she's good at poker, don't play with her."

Cat eyed me. "What do you mean about that?"

"People who play it close to the chest like she does all the time are probably pretty good at not letting anyone know when they have a good hand. Got to be careful."

"I don't think I'm good at poker," she announced.

"Should we practice?"

At Cat's nod, I fetched a deck of cards out of the drawer by the couch, and we began playing.

We were a few hands in when she asked, "Do you miss Mom?"

I looked up quickly. "Of course, I do."

Out of all of us, Cat spoke about Mom the least. I was pretty sure she missed her the most. I figured losing someone you loved was a relative experience in a sense. The way it was for me might not be the way it was for someone else. Cat had been the youngest, and she'd also carried more of the brunt of our dad. Flynn had a different dad from us, but his dad had simply been gone. He'd knocked up our mom, and that was it. She'd never heard from him again. I didn't know what was worse.

Later, when our dad's health started to fail, and he needed our mom, he hung around more. That meant more arguments and more drinking. Nora and I had been a little older. Not that it had been easy, but we'd managed. He'd scared Cat, and we all knew it.

"I'll always miss Mom," I added. When she looked up quickly, I saw the sheen of tears in her eyes. "You okay?"

Her lips twisted. Her voice was a little thick when she spoke. "I've just been thinking about her lately. I'm eighteen now, and she's not here." She swung her arm in an arc. "She didn't get to see that you guys built this. She didn't get to see everything Flynn and you did."

A tear rolled down her cheek, and she swiped it away quickly. Cat did not like to be hugged when she was crying, so I waited.

"And, now I'm all grown up. She doesn't even get to taste the food that I cook."

"No, she doesn't," I said, my throat feeling tight.

"I wish you'd been here."

"What do you mean?" I prompted.

"I understand why you went to college, but I missed you. It was so scary that night when she collapsed."

I took a quick breath. I knew Cat wasn't trying to guilt me, but I still felt like hell about it.

"I know. I wish I'd been there too."

"It wouldn't have changed anything," my little sister said softly.

I nodded. I'd mentally replayed what the doctor at the emergency room had told us the next day. He said we couldn't have stopped it. She had hypertrophic cardiomyopathy, something that caused the heart muscles to thicken and could occasionally disrupt the heart's electrical system and result in sudden death. Even though I'd intellectually believed the doctor, I harbored emotional doubts.

"I know," I said, my voice ragged on the edges.

"Nora and I weren't doing too great."

"Nora was sixteen. She hated life," I offered.

Cat giggled a little and swiped another tear away. "Thanks," she said quietly.

"For what?"

"For always being there."

"I wasn't there that night," I pointed out.

"No, but you drove down from Anchorage in the dark and met us at the hospital. You convinced the court to let you be our guardian until Flynn could get here."

It had taken Flynn weeks to get back. He was across the world on active duty in the Air Force at the time. As a young college kid, the judge had had his doubts about me. Having grown up in the area, I had several people support me, including a friend of our mom's who promised to check on us regularly. They allowed me to be the temporary guardian until Flynn could get home. After that, I stayed home. I'd eventually finished my college degree, but in fits and starts with most of it online. I hadn't been able to bring myself to leave after that and hadn't wanted to.

"What if one of us has that?" Cat asked.

"We don't. We've all been checked since," I pointed out.

She took a breath. "I know, but I worry." After a beat, she added, as if to herself, "All right, I'm done with this conversation."

That was classic Cat. She didn't like being hugged when she was crying, and when she was done with a heavy topic, she just wanted to move on. We continued playing cards.

After I went to bed later and I knew Cat was in her room, I knocked lightly on the wall between my bedroom and Harley's. A moment later, my door opened, and Harley tiptoed into the room.

Chapter Sixteen

HARLEY

"Here you go." Gemma handed me a glass of water.

I was seated in her kitchen on a stool at the counter with my feet hooked around the rungs. "Thank you." I took a swallow, glancing out the windows.

Gemma had purchased this home with Diego. The house came with horses, and I watched one of them nibbling grass along the edge of the fence. The home sat on a rise, offering a view of Kachemak Bay in the distance through the trees. Sunshine glittered on the surface of the water, the wind ruffling it and creating little sparks of light.

Looking back toward Gemma, I watched as she stirred meat in a pan. She was making tacos. She had invited me over for dinner with her and Diego, something she did fairly often.

She glanced over, casting me a quick smile.

"What?" I asked.

"Just thinking I'm glad you are who you are," she replied.

"Same." I loved Gemma, and she was perfect for my brother.

She turned the flame down under the pan, setting a lid on it, and turned around to face me. She smoothed a hand over her rumpled, honey-blond curls, her eyes sparkling with her smile.

After a second, her gaze sobered. "I invited you over early because Diego's worried."

"Worried?" I interjected.

She sighed. "Yes."

Even though she didn't spell it out, I knew she was referring to his concern about my health. "It's fine. I have a minor heart issue."

Gemma's brow furrowed, her concerned gaze skating over my face. "A minor heart problem? You're pretty young for a heart problem."

I shrugged, ignoring the nervous feeling in my belly. "Apparently, there's a family history of it."

"But what is it?"

"It's this thing where sometimes my heart goes too fast or skips a beat. It's called supraventricular tachy-cardia or SVT."

Gemma nodded slowly. "Okay, so what does it mean?"

"Well, if it's happening, and if I get up too quickly or something like that, I might faint. That's what Grant saw. But it's fine," I insisted. "I haven't fainted that many times."

"How many times?" Gemma pressed. She pushed away from the counter, crossing over to slide her hips onto a stool across from where I was sitting at the island.

She looked way too worried for my comfort level. "It's really not much, I swear. Have you ever fainted?"

"Yeah. Heat stroke one summer."

"Oh, really?"

"We traveled to the beach on the East Coast. I wasn't used to the humidity."

"See, fainting happens," I said, striving to keep my tone nonchalant.

She cocked her head to the side. "You know, I'm giving you a dry run."

"What?"

"A dry run. Diego is going to show up, and you could use some practice." She glanced at her watch. "He'll be here in about fifteen minutes. He's going to ask you all the same questions. I know you don't want him to worry, but it'd be best if you're honest. Is there anything we can help with?"

"I do *not* need help," I ground out.

Gemma lifted her hands, letting them fall lightly on the counter. "I didn't say you did, but Diego wants to help."

"There's nothing he can do." I took another gulp of water, willing the churning in my stomach to slow down.

"So is that the whole story?"

"Yes," I lied.

I wasn't about to tell her that Quinn recommended I take medication. I didn't want to take medication. I wanted to just manage it. It wasn't that I was opposed to medicine in general. Just not for me.

Gemma studied me quietly. "What does Quinn think?"

I lied again. "He's prescribed some medication, and I'll start soon."

Just then, we heard the door to the front of the house opening. Gemma glanced at me, her lips twitching with a smile.

"Thanks for the practice," I teased.

"He's early."

"You knew he would be. He's ready to grill me."

She snorted a laugh.

Diego appeared a moment later, tossing his backpack in a closet. As he shrugged out of his jacket and kicked his boots off, he called over, "Hey!"

Gemma slipped off the stool and crossed over to him. "Hey there. Dinner should be ready soon."

For a moment, I might as well have been invisible. Diego dipped his head, giving her a lingering kiss. I looked away, feeling a pang in my chest. Their intimacy was so evident that it was almost its own force.

My mind skipped over to Grant, and I immediately shoved him out of the way. I did *not* need to be dwelling on hot nights with Grant while having dinner with my brother.

A moment later, Gemma returned to the stove to check on the meat. Diego opened the refrigerator and fetched a bottle of beer. He turned to face me as he removed the cap and tossed it in the wastebasket.

"Hey, how was your day?" I asked.

After finishing a swallow of his beer, he crossed over, sitting on the stool Gemma had just vacated. "Pretty good. Busy."

"You're always busy."

"I could say the same about you," he replied.

I shrugged. "I like it that way."

"So do I," he teased after another swallow of his beer.

I called over to Gemma, "Do you need me to do anything?"

She glanced over, shaking her head. "Nope. Everything's already prepped." My gaze scanned the counter where she had prepared small bowls of taco fixings. "I'm putting the soft shells in the oven right now."

"I am freaking starving," Diego announced when he put his beer bottle on the counter.

"You're in luck. Gemma's cooking you dinner," I teased.

Gemma called over, "He cooks as much as I do."

"I know he does. He's a good man."

When I glanced toward Diego, he had a familiar focused look in his eyes, studying me.

"What?" I asked automatically.

"What's up with you fainting?"

I sighed. "Didn't Terese tell you?"

"Yeah, she said it's a heart thing our aunt had and not to get too worried."

"Well, don't worry then. That should be enough information for you," I countered.

Diego narrowed his eyes. "Harley..." he began.

"Just because I'm your little sister doesn't mean I'm required to give you a blow-by-blow."

"Did you tell Gemma?"

"Fine. It's a thing where my heartbeat can be irregular and sometimes skips a beat. That's it."

"What does that mean? Grant said you fainted."

"I did. I think that night it was because I hadn't eaten anything. Combining that with this, I fainted."

"How many times have you fainted?"

"Oh my God," I muttered. "Not many. So few I haven't kept count."

I was lying. I knew exactly how many times I'd fainted—six times. I was not about to offer more details to my overprotective brother.

"What did Quinn say?"

"I have an appointment with him next week to talk about a medication recommendation."

"Can I talk to him?"

"No. Diego, it's not necessary for you to talk to him."

I *really* didn't want him talking to my doctor. That just felt weird.

Gemma swooped in. "Time for dinner," she said as she set a bowl filled with taco meat in front of us. She turned to get the taco shells out of the oven.

"Are they going to be crispy?" I asked.

She shook her head as she lifted them with a spatula onto a plate.

Diego didn't get the memo. "It's just your regular doctor, not your OBGYN."

I rolled my eyes. "Diego, if it becomes necessary for you to talk to my doctor, you can talk to my doctor. This is not an emergency."

He lifted his beer and took a swallow before replying, "Promise me you'll keep me in the loop."

"Absolutely." I would keep him in the loop. I just wouldn't tell him the whole story.

Chapter Seventeen

HARLEY

A full week had passed since my first night with Grant. Since then, we'd spent a few stolen hours together every night. We mostly used my bedroom because it was a little farther away from Cat's, which was directly across the hall from Grant's room. Grant would spend a few hours with me before getting up early and slipping back into his bedroom. I even noticed that he was going out of his way to leave his bed unmade so Cat wouldn't suspect anything.

That made the whole thing feel even more sneaky. I secretly loved it. I was coming to crave my skin-to-skin time with him. Yet it was doing absolutely nothing to achieve my goal of burning him out of my system.

I kept telling myself I wasn't going to catch feelings for him. I couldn't help the thrill of anticipation that sizzled through me when I opened the door Friday and found him alone on the couch.

"Where's Cat?" I asked.

He glanced my way, and the heat banked in his

gaze sent my belly into a wild flip. "She's staying in town tonight with a friend."

"Oh."

I felt the burn of his gaze on me as I hung my jacket up and kicked off my shoes. My purse fell to the floor with a thud.

Every night with him had been fiery hot, and now we didn't have to keep it quiet. All that pent-up tension was like an engine revving too hard and fast in my body.

As soon as I began crossing the room, he stood from the couch. We reached each other in two strides. His hand slid into my hair as he dipped his head and fit his mouth over mine. Our kiss combusted. Sparks and smoke practically flew from the force of the explosion. We were hungry for each other, near frantic as we tugged at each other's clothes.

"Fuck, Harley," he groaned.

I unbuttoned his jeans, quickly sliding my palm down. I was greedy to feel him. My hand closed around his velvety-hot length, and I shifted my thighs, already wet and needy for him.

"Well, that's the point, isn't it?" I murmured as I strung kisses across his now bare chest.

His throaty chuckle sent tingles spinning like little pinwheels of sparks over my skin. I needed to taste him. Impatient, I shoved his jeans and boxers down at once, and his cock sprang free.

I leaned over, swirling my tongue around the tip, savoring the salty tang of his cum. His fingers laced in my hair, and the sting on my scalp spun into the rest of the sensations stampeding through my body.

"Fuck, sweetheart. Not yet," he growled.

My mouth closed around him, and I sucked him in deeply. His hand fisted more tightly in my hair as I curled my palm around his wet length, letting it slide up and down. I teased him with my mouth and tongue, sucking deeply again.

"Harley..." He let out a groan just before his cum spurted into my mouth.

"I was impatient," I explained as I rose up, swiping my tongue across my bottom lip.

Grant's eyes darkened. "Your turn," he murmured in a low whisper.

He spun me around. He'd already divested me of my shirt, and he trailed his knuckles lightly along the lace edge of my bra. My nipples tightened in anticipation. A moment later, cool air hit them as he undid the clasp and pushed my bra off my shoulders.

"Hmm, where should I start?" His fingers trailed down the side of my neck, sending goose bumps prickling over the surface of my skin.

His touch was as light as air and barely a whisper, but it felt like flames licking over my skin. That fiery touch trailed down, teasing one nipple and then the other as he watched me. My channel was clenching.

"Grant," I begged.

"Oh, no, sweetheart. You bought yourself a ticket to me taking my time I need to get ready for round two."

My mouth fell open with a little gasp when he lightly pinched a nipple. His mouth followed, closing around my nipple and giving a sharp suck. I cried out. Even the feel of his low chuckle on my skin was yet another sensation, something else to amp up the need driving me.

He teased my breasts, my thoughts blurring as fierce desire rushed through me. He hadn't even unbuttoned my jeans yet. I started to get impatient and reached between us, but he pushed my hands away.

"That's for me."

I was acquainted with Grant's maddening tendency to drag things out. I knew what lay at the end of this torture—an explosive, body-shattering orgasm.

So I acquiesced. By the time he finally unbuttoned my jeans and shoved them down over my hips, my panties were drenched. He pushed them to the side, teasing his fingers in my folds, murmuring, "Just for me."

I bit my lip, trying to keep from crying out. Another moment later, he had me stretched out on the couch and was pushing my knees apart. I felt the subtle burn of his stubble when he dropped hot kisses on the inside of each thigh. He finally, *finally*, brought his mouth to my sex.

My hips bucked into him instantly. He already knew me well. He knew just what to do to bring me to the edge. He fucked me slow and sure with his fingers while his tongue teased me to near incoherence. A flash of pleasure finally burst in a ray through my body. My mind went blank as I cried out, and the orgasm hit me in deep waves with the pleasure running through so forcefully that I was nearly limp.

By the time he rose up, I dragged my eyes open, propping myself on my elbows to see him kicking his jeans free of his ankles. His arousal jutted out. He turned, sitting on the couch and murmuring, "Come 'ere. I know you like to ride me."

I did. That said, Grant inside me any which way was amazing. But this was just perfect. Somehow, I gathered enough muscle coordination to straddle him. On the heels of a breath, he was filling me. He controlled my descent, and the delicious feel of him stretching me elicited a deep moan.

My forehead fell to his, and he kissed me, slow and light. He gripped my hips and thrust, filling me completely. The pressure where we were joined created a pleasure so intense, I had to bite my lip to keep from coming again.

"Sweetheart, you don't have to wait. I'm right there with you," Grant murmured against my lips.

One more thrust and the slippery pressure over my clit sent me spiraling again as I cried out. I loved that he said my name on the heels of a ragged shout. The heat of his release filled me, satisfying in a way I didn't even understand.

I curled against him, and he simply held me there on the couch. I could feel his heart beating against mine. Our breathing slowed together. His fingers sifted through my hair, and I loved it. This was the part I was starting to worry about.

Oh, the sex was amazing. Beyond amazing. I just wasn't supposed to feel so good being held by him. It felt exactly right.

As the youngest in my family, I had always fought to show that no one needed to worry about me. I fought to be independent, fought to be strong. As a result, I hated to feel vulnerable. Yet with Grant, I did.

It frightened me because my usual inclination to fight against it when we were together like this dissipated into nothing.

"Do you think that was too loud?" he asked.

I giggled against his neck where my head was tucked. I lifted it, meeting his eyes. "It doesn't matter. Cat's not here. Is she gone all weekend?" I asked, not even bothering to keep the hopeful tone out of my voice.

"I don't know. Definitely tonight. Nora dropped her off."

"Ah, so we should christen every room in the house while we have time."

Grant chuckled. "Well, we've already taken care of the kitchen, now the living room, the stairs, your bedroom, and my bedroom. I'm sorry, but my sister's bedroom is off-limits for me. But there's the bathroom."

He waggled his eyebrows, and I giggled again. A teeny-tiny voice, like the kind you hear from a great distance, tried to shout out in my mind that I should be worried. This was supposed to feel awkward, but it didn't. I ignored it.

Chapter Eighteen

GRANT

Cat was gone again the next night. We'd already christened the bathroom, so to speak. I'd fucked Harley long and slow against the tiled wall. Twice. She'd also given me a morning blow job in there.

Things between us were getting dicey, and I knew it. Yet it was just too good. I couldn't *not* give in to my need for her. I savored the way she was when we were naked. When she had her clothes on, her armor was on, but once we were bare, she let her guard down. I loved every second of it.

It made me feel like there might be something there for both of us. My cynical mind was all, *What the fuck, dude?*

"Dude, you're like seriously zoning out," Flynn offered a few days later from where he sat on a stool beside me at the counter in the lodge kitchen. "What are you thinking about?"

"Nothing," I lied.

Telling Flynn what I was thinking about was definitely a bad plan. Flynn was my brother, and he was also my friend. And Diego was one of his best friends.

All the guys who worked here were his best friends. If Flynn knew what I was doing with Diego's little sister and Diego found out, there'd be hell to pay.

"Not much, just seriously zoning out," I added.

Flynn knew me well enough to know better, but he let me bullshit and simply shrugged. Daphne was pulling a tray out of the oven. A moment later, she was sliding some rolls onto a plate. "Help yourself, guys."

"Oh, what are they?" I asked.

"Guess," she teased.

"Are they too hot to eat now?"

"Hell, yeah," Flynn said. "I have learned this lesson. We have to wait a few minutes."

"Do you know what they are?"

He shook his head.

"Let's bet on the guess."

"Sure, five bucks to who's right," he agreed.

A few minutes later, Flynn and I both bit into a roll. I spoke first, "Onion, spinach, and I think that's mozzarella."

Flynn chewed and swallowed. "My guess is onion, spinach, and muenster cheese."

Daphne's eyes were twinkling as she glanced back and forth between us. "Grant is right."

"About what?" Diego called as he entered the kitchen from the back door, catching the last comment.

"Grant guessed the filling," Flynn replied. "I don't have any cash on me right now. I promise I'll give it to you later."

I snorted. "You'll forget."

"No way," Flynn insisted.

"You probably will," Diego said as he slipped his hips onto the stool beside me.

"Hey, I don't usually forget," Flynn protested.

"Yeah, you do," Diego and I said in unison.

Flynn looked affronted. "I'm going to get some cash now."

Daphne grinned as he stood and strode quickly to the back door.

"Can I have one?" Diego asked.

"You don't need to ask," Daphne said as she handed him a small plate.

Diego snagged one of the rolls from the serving plate in front of us. "How's it going?" he asked.

"Pretty good," I replied. "What are you doing out here tonight?"

"It's yoga night, man."

"Oh, that's right. I forgot."

"Better not forget. You know Gemma takes that real personally," he said somberly.

"She does not," Daphne countered. "Although I expect everyone to show up. I love yoga class with Gemma."

I shifted my shoulders. "I always get tension right back here." I reached up and patted below my neck, just between my shoulder blades.

"Well, if you go to yoga enough, you can actually reach down there," Diego offered dryly.

Daphne went into the pantry to get something, returning and busying herself at the stove. "Where's Cat?" I asked.

"She's going in for a tryout with the theater in town," Daphne replied.

"Oh, really?"

"Yep. She said she'll probably spend the night with her friend because the tryouts run late."

"Oh, wow. I think that'll be fun for her. What will you do if she gets a part?" I asked.

"She said that practice is only during the week

until they have the show. The show is scheduled for three weekends. We'll survive without her."

Of course, my brain immediately realized if that happened, I'd get more freedom with Harley on the nights that Cat wasn't home. I kicked those thoughts to the curb swiftly. I did *not* need to be fantasizing about Harley with her older brother sitting beside me.

"Thanks for telling me what happened with Harley by the way," he offered. "She talked to me about it the other night."

"Yeah?"

"Yeah. Sounds like it's gonna be okay. She went to the doctor. She said Quinn will prescribe her some medication and that it's pretty minor," Diego explained.

"Well, good." I was relieved myself.

What are you doing, dude?

As it was, I didn't want to worry about her. It was enough to be hiding this secret.

"What's going on with Harley?" Daphne asked.

"Minor heart condition. I guess she occasionally has an irregular heartbeat," Diego replied.

"Is that a big deal?" Daphne pressed.

"She says it's not. I guess one of our aunts has the same issue. I only know because Grant let me know she fainted. She's still a little pissed about it," Diego offered.

"People are kind of private about health stuff, and Harley doesn't like people worrying about her," Daphne said.

"Yeah, for God's sake, don't tell her I mentioned it," Diego said with a shake of his head.

Just then, Harley walked into the kitchen, glancing around. "Are you guys talking about me?"

"Oh, fuck," Diego muttered.

Daphne cast her a warm smile. "Don't worry. He was just thanking Grant for letting him know you fainted."

Harley narrowed her eyes. "It's fine. It's not a secret. Not anymore. Thanks to Grant and now you," she said pointedly.

"Hey, what did I do?" Diego countered.

"Well, I know Grant wouldn't bring it up again," she retorted.

I was actually relieved she said that. "I didn't, I swear." I held both of my palms up.

Harley's cheeks were flushed when she sat down at the counter at an angle across from me. I ignored the jolt of awareness. So much for the stupid idea that this would burn out between us. Not even close. The chemistry between us was on a repeating circuit, burning hotter by the day.

"Most everyone has something going on with their health," Daphne offered.

"What's your deal then?" Harley countered. She sighed when Daphne shrugged. "Thanks for trying to make me feel better."

Diego glanced at his sister, his brow furrowing. "I'm sorry, I shouldn't have brought it up."

"It's okay. It's all out in the open now. You know, Gemma knows, Daphne knows, Grant knows. It's not a big deal. Can we change the subject, please?"

"Sure, have a roll," Diego said, sliding the plate by with the savory rolls closer to her.

She grabbed one just as Daphne set a small plate in front of her. "Oh my God, these are so good," she said after a bite.

"They're so good. We all talk with our mouths full," Diego teased.

Flynn reappeared with a five-dollar bill in hand. As

he slapped it down in front of me on the counter, he asked, "Do I owe you anything else?"

I shook my head. He looked at Diego, who did the same. "You finally paid me after losing at poker a couple of weeks ago."

"Oh, are we having girls' card night soon?" Harley asked, gesturing in Daphne's direction.

"Just the girls?" Diego asked as he looked at Harley.

"Yes, you guys did guys' night for a while, so it's girls' night because there are more women in the staff house now."

The door to the hallway opened again, this time with Gemma appearing. "Girls' card night," Daphne called over.

"Where?" Gemma asked as she walked over, stopping between Harley and Diego and leaning over to press a kiss on his cheek.

He slid his arm around her waist and pulled her close. "Can I come?"

"No," Gemma replied with a smile.

"It's at the staff house whenever we do it," Harley offered. "Cat's been practicing with Grant."

"I'm good at poker," Daphne said.

"You are?" Diego asked.

She nodded. "Oh, yes."

"Let's just play for fun," Gemma interjected.

"Why don't you invite the guys?" Diego persisted.

"No," Harley said, narrowing her eyes.

He rested his forehead on Gemma's shoulder as she chuckled. He lifted his head and gave her a lingering kiss. I looked away. The intimacy and closeness between them were so obvious. My heart clenched as I reflexively glanced toward Harley. She was looking down at her plate. Her eyes lifted, colliding with mine, and I experienced a jolt. It felt as if the air between us sparked. She looked down quickly, and I grabbed another roll, taking a big bite.

Fuck me. It was getting harder and harder to be around her in front of our friends.

Chapter Nineteen

HARLEY

The following evening, I got back to the staff house before Grant, which wasn't unusual. I usually got here first. Sometimes I had dinner at the lodge, but I often came back and worked after eating a little early. I needed the quiet to focus.

I was in the kitchen making some tea when my heart felt funny. I ignored the sensation, pouring a generous dollop of honey into my tea and taking a swallow. As I turned to walk across the kitchen, I felt light-headed and fuzzy and knew what was about to happen. I felt myself slipping.

I came to a few minutes later. I glanced up at the clock. Eight minutes had passed since I walked into the kitchen. I felt shaky and wanted to rest on the floor, yet I was galvanized to get myself up. Grant might arrive at any minute.

On unsteady legs, I scrambled to my feet, scanning the floor. My tea had fallen. The mug was broken, and tea had spilled on the floor. Blessedly, I hadn't landed in the spilled tea or

any of the shards from the mug. I hurried to the

sink, grabbing the paper towels from the corner of the counter. A moment later, I was sweeping up the glass when I heard the front door open.

"Fuck!" I hissed to myself.

"What?" Grant called.

"Oh, nothing," I called in return.

Of course, the man had long legs and crossed from the living room area into the kitchen in maybe one second. He stood in the archway between the rooms, surveying the kitchen floor. I had the dustpan in hand. His eyes landed on the shards of the mug.

"What happened?"

"I dropped my tea. I walked too quickly, and it sloshed over. It was hot, so I dropped it," I lied.

Grant looked at me suspiciously, but he nodded. "Okay." After a beat, he pressed, "Tell me the truth."

"I am. I swear." I felt a pinch of guilt, the sting sharp in my heart.

He was quiet for a long moment. "It's not like you owe me anything, but my mom died from a heart defect that we didn't know she had."

That stinging sensation burned more deeply. Grant's shoulders rose and fell with a deep breath. He closed his eyes for a moment. I reflexively crossed the kitchen to him, still holding the dustpan.

"I'm sorry," I said.

His eyes opened. "It's not your fault."

"I know. That's not how I meant it. I'm sorry in general that she died. I didn't know how she died."

"We all got tested for it after that," he added. "None of us have it."

"I have SVT," I blurted out. I quickly explained what it was to him, ending with, "Just a weird heart thing. Sometimes my heart skips a beat or gets irregular. That's why I faint sometimes. I'm following up with Quinn next week to discuss medication."

Grant nodded slowly before his eyes shifted down to the dustpan. "You should put that in the trash."

I rolled my eyes. "I will." I quickly brushed the remaining shards from the mug into the dustpan and dumped it in the trash before walking to the closet in the corner of the kitchen and pulling out the mop. "There was honey in my tea," I explained over my shoulder.

After I mopped, I asked, "Where's Cat?"

"I guess she's staying in town."

I bit my lip as I felt heat race into my cheeks. My pulse vroomed faster. "Are you sure she's spending the night in town?"

"Yes. Nora dropped her off. She's at practice tonight."

"Should we watch TV?" I asked.

"Sure."

This was all for show. We were just going through the motions. I knew, in a matter of minutes, we wouldn't be able to keep our hands off each other. In a way, I wanted the tease of it. The anticipation itself was becoming addictive with Grant. Hiding it from Cat was almost overwhelming. The secrecy created this undercurrent of need and the thrill of the forbidden every night. By the time the coast was clear —meaning Cat had been in her room long enough that we could guess she had gone to sleep—Grant would open his bedroom door. He would go into the bathroom, wait a minute or two before flushing the toilet, and fake opening and closing his door again. Only then would he stealthily enter my room.

We would lose ourselves in each other. Sometimes

it was rushed, and sometimes it was slow. We were *always* quiet.

A little while later, I was sitting a few feet away from him on the couch. He glanced over, reaching for my hand and placing it over his arousal. I was wet, and I couldn't help but bite my lip and let out a little moan as my channel clenched with need.

"Tell me how wet you are," he murmured, low under his breath.

I shifted my hips before unbuttoning my jeans and shimmying them down with one hand just far enough to give him access. "Why don't you find out?"

He moved closer to me on the couch. My eyes fluttered closed, and I whimpered when he slipped his fingers into me.

"Fuck me," he murmured.

I was soaked, slippery wet. He slid two fingers inside, stretching me before sliding them out. I whimpered in protest. He lifted his hand, sucking his fingers into his mouth. His eyes were locked to mine when he drew them out. "I fucking love how you taste."

In a flash, we were frantic, tearing at each other's clothes. My climax couldn't come fast enough as I straddled him, sheathing him inside me swiftly. I came in a noisy burst just before he thrust upward one final time. The cords in his neck were standing out as his hands gripped my hips tightly. He came with my name on his lips in a husky whisper.

I collapsed against him. He held me tight to him for a few breaths before he tensed. Lifting my head, I saw his eyes go wide. "I hear someone."

We scrambled apart swiftly. I didn't know how, but we got our clothes on in a matter of seconds. I raced into the kitchen to button my shirt with my back to the door as it burst open.

"Hey!" Cat called.

"Hey," Grant said, his voice all low and casual.

He had the remote in hand and was flicking through the channels. His cheeks had a subtle flush, but he appeared completely composed. I turned the faucet on, rinsing my hands under the cold water to ease the heat still burning through me. "Hey!" I called over my shoulder, giving myself just enough time to cool off.

"I thought you were at practice for the play," I said a moment later as I returned to the living room.

Cat was hanging up her jacket and taking her shoes off. "Practice ended early because one of the leads is sick. We just did our run-throughs."

"I thought Nora dropped you off," Grant said.

Cat nodded. "My friend brought me home. Her house is a little past the turnoff to our road. My friend's boyfriend was spending the night, so I didn't want to cramp her style. What are you watching?" she asked as she plunked down on the couch.

"As usual, Grant can't decide," I teased lightly.

Grant rolled his eyes. I grabbed my laptop off the table in the corner of the living room and sat down on the couch at an angle across from him.

Cat glanced over. "We're on for Friday, right?"

"Yep. Do you have practice then?"

"We only practice during the week until the week before. Then it's every night with only one night off a week until the show is over."

"Do we get tickets?" I asked.

"Of course! You're all coming, right?"

"Hell yeah. I cannot wait," Grant said.

———

The following morning, I was in the kitchen emptying the dishwasher when I heard Grant's footsteps on the stairs. I didn't even want to contemplate how well I knew the pace of his walk. Cat had already left to go over to the lodge. I would be following her shortly. I knew Grant would as well because he never wanted to miss breakfast there. The stolen hours with Grant last night had been a haze of passion and need.

It was starting to feel as though the very secrecy itself was binding us closer and closer to each other. It was just us in the darkness, skin to skin and tangled together. I felt my pulse start to race. I took a quick breath, ordering myself to ignore it. Except knowing that Cat was gone, a tiny little corner of me wanted to take advantage

I forced myself to continue my task, except there was no denying my body's awareness of his potent presence. A shiver chased down my spine and tingles spread throughout my body.

"Hey, hey," he murmured, coming up behind me.

He dipped his head and pressed a lingering kiss on the back of my neck. Goose bumps rose on the surface of my skin, and my breath became short instantly.

"Hey." My voice came out husky with a rasp to it.

Turning, I found myself caged between his arms when he rested each hand on the edges of the counter beside my hips. His eyes skated over my face.

"You headed to the lodge?" he asked. His voice was low and gravelly. It got to me every time. Now that I knew what he sounded like with my name on a ragged, whispered shout when he came, all he had to do was speak, and it sent fire spinning through my veins.

"Uh-huh." That was all I could manage before he bent low, his lips meeting mine.

His kiss started gentle, just a brushing touch. But

then, he lingered, dropping a kiss at one corner and then the other. I was breathless and needy by the time he fully fit his mouth over mine.

I lost track of time. It couldn't have been more than a moment or two before the front door swung open abruptly. It was too late because there was a wide archway between the living room and the kitchen, offering a direct line of sight from the door to where we were pinned against the counter. If we hadn't been in the middle of kissing, we would have heard Cat's footsteps likely pounding up the stairs.

She came to a skidding stop, letting out a gasp of surprise followed with, "Oh wow."

Grant and I broke apart. He turned. "Wow, what?" he asked, his tone all casual.

Meanwhile, my cheeks were burning up.

"You're kissing," Cat pointed out as she strode across the living room into the kitchen.

I wanted to lie and play it off, but I knew we couldn't.

"So what?" Grant countered with an easy shrug.

I met Cat's eyes, scrambling to think of what to say. "Could you maybe keep this to yourself?" I finally asked.

Cat's calculating gaze bounced between us before she finally held my eyes and nodded. "Only for you."

"Cat," Grant said, his tone edged with a warning.

"What? I'm only keeping it between us for Harley's sake. Not yours," she returned pointedly.

"What are you doing here?" he asked, choosing to ignore that.

"I left my phone in my bedroom."

"Well then, why are you here in the kitchen?"

"Because I walked in, and you two were totally making out," she replied with a sly grin.

Grant rolled his eyes. I took a deep breath.

Cat looked my way. "I won't say anything, but we're talking later."

At that, she spun away, walking briskly out of the living room and sprinting up the stairs. A moment later, she was already pounding down them, calling out, "Your secret's safe with me!"

Grant and I were left staring at each other in the kitchen when the door slammed behind her.

"Fuck," he muttered.

"Nothing to do about it now," I said, trying to keep my tone light. "I honestly don't care who knows except for Diego."

"Well, you know he's gonna find out."

"Cat won't tell anybody," I countered.

"You think? I love my sister, and I'm sure she will try to keep it quiet for your sake, but that will only hold for a little while."

"What should we do?" I asked.

I knew the easy answer. We should stop fooling around. Right now. Except I didn't want to stop.

"Should we stop?" he asked.

"Do you want to?" I returned, my heart kicking faster in my chest.

"No," he said after the silence stretched too long. "Do you?"

My cheeks burned hot again as I shook my head.

"Okay then."

He stepped closer, pulling me back into his arms. I loved the feel of him—warm, strong. He felt like someone I could lean on. When we were together, I always felt good. It was when we were apart that I worried and got anxious. I didn't like how I was starting to rely on him. I didn't like how I felt safe with him, which was a paradox.

His forehead fell to mine, and he whispered, "I'll see you tonight." His lips moved against mine with each word just before he gave me a lingering kiss.

He straightened, asking, "Should we walk over together?"

I almost shook my head, but the thing was, we had walked over together many times. I shrugged and resisted the urge to reach for his hand every step of the way.

Chapter Twenty

GRANT

Several days passed with the tension high between Harley and me whenever we were around anyone else. We still adhered to the silent agreement that nothing happened until Cat was in her bedroom for a solid hour or more. The tension ratcheted higher when we were with Cat in the staff house. She thought it was funny. She was enjoying being in on a secret. She was enjoying it enough that I thought she would actually keep her word. I knew she would try, but she would likely slip up at some point.

The worry about that was eating at me. Late one afternoon, I landed after a busy day of supply delivery mixed in with a few tourist trips. I walked into what most of us thought of as the main plane hangar for Walker Adventures. We used several here, but this was the one where we had an office.

Diego was there, tinkering in the engine compartment of one of the planes.

"What's the problem?" I called over as I approached.

He glanced over his shoulder and shrugged. "I'm probably going to need to give Ryan a call."

Like my brother and the other pilots, Diego could handle the basic mechanical issues for planes. They'd all been in the Air Force together and had taught me some mechanics, but I wasn't as good as them. Ryan was a local guy who had gotten his training in airplane mechanics and had a lot more time than we did to handle issues.

"I keep having this problem with one of the valves. We need a full replacement. He's got the time, and I don't," Diego pointed out.

Diego straightened, catching my eyes. He and Harley shared the same deep-green eyes. My chest pinched with a twinge of guilt. I knew she didn't want Diego to know what was happening with us, but I was struggling with my thoughts about it. It was inevitable he would find out. I'd rather just own it than have him find out another way.

"What's up?" he asked. He was a perceptive guy and sensed something was off kilter with me. He reached up, lowering the small hood to the engine and closing it.

I paused, tension tightening in my gut. "Look, I need to tell you something." I gulped in air.

The thing was, I had feelings for Harley. I sensed I wasn't alone in that. I knew we'd planned for this to burn out, but that wasn't happening. Not even close. I was far past convincing myself she was just a friend, and I didn't want this to blow up in my face.

I figured maybe I could thread the needle here. I didn't have to tell Diego we were hooking up. I could tell him I had feelings for Harley and see where that went.

"You got a minute?" I asked.

"Standing right in front of you," he said with a chuckle, "and I just asked you what was up. Of course, I have a minute. Something bothering you?"

"You're probably gonna kick my ass," I finally said, deciding to take the most direct approach.

His brows hitched up, his eyes narrowing. "This about Harley?"

"Uh, yeah. I have feelings for her."

Fuck, that sounded weird.

His eyes narrowed further. "Uh, okay. You acted on those feelings?" he pressed.

I shook my head, deciding to keep my lies silent. "I just wanted to let you know about it before it became a thing."

Diego studied me. It felt like his gaze was boring into my very soul. "You telling me the whole story?" His tone was understandably skeptical.

"I just told you I have feelings for your sister. That's the story." I deliberately dropped "whole" from that, but whatever.

Diego eyed me quietly before nodding slowly. "Okay."

"Okay, what?" I pressed.

"Just okay."

"Well, are you upset with me?"

"Of course, I am. She's my little sister."

"She's an adult," I heard myself pointing out.

"Obviously, she can do what she wants, but you're a good guy, and I trust you with my life when it comes to flying and working together. But you don't exactly have a great reputation when it comes to women. Casual is the name of your game."

I swallowed. He was entirely accurate on that.

"But—" I began.

"But what? How will it be different with my sister?"

"Because I care about her."

He looked at me like I was a dumbass, which, when it came to Harley, I was. "Look, I'm not going to be stupid. I know if I tell you to stay the fuck away from her, that's gonna make you, I guess, have more feelings for her. And I'm pretty sure you're not telling me the whole fucking story. Whatever you do, don't fucking hurt her."

"I would never do that."

"Sometimes we hurt people when we don't intend to hurt them. You know?"

I nodded. "Of course." He had me there. "So do you want to kick my ass?" I finally asked.

"If you hurt her, I *will* kick your ass."

At that, he turned and walked away. "I gotta go," he tossed over his shoulder.

I watched as he walked out of the plane hangar. It was just then I realized Tucker was in the office. I heard his footsteps as he approached. "Hey," I said, feeling glum.

Tucker met my gaze as he approached, smiling slowly. "So that went well."

I groaned. "Yeah." I leaned against the plane, scuffing the toe of my boot against the concrete.

He chuckled. "So, uh, you have feelings for Harley?"

I rolled my eyes. "Yeah, I do."

"That definitely isn't the whole story," he pointed out.

"Oh, for fuck's sake, dude."

He threw his head back with a hearty laugh. When he leveled his eyes with mine again, his gaze sobered. "What *is* going on?"

"I like her."

"It's never that simple, dude."

"I know. Fuck, I've never had feelings for anyone." I scrubbed a hand through my hair.

"I know the feeling."

"What do you mean? You're in love with Skylar. You two are doing great. Plus, you had that girlfriend in high school."

Tucker had been in love in high school, and his girlfriend died. He simply nodded. "I suppose you're right. But, dude, it's never easy. If this is the first time you've wanted more than a hookup, well, it'll be terrifying."

"What should I do?"

He cast me a sympathetic smile. "I do not have an easy answer."

"It's complicated because Diego is kind of like an older brother to me."

"Yeah, and Harley's his younger sister. This isn't going to be a neat and tidy situation. If you hurt Harley, he'll probably kick your ass."

"I'll let him," I offered.

Tucker laughed softly. "Good man."

"Are you done flying for the day?" I asked.

He nodded. I glanced at my watch. "Want to go grab dinner somewhere?"

"Dude, it's yoga night."

"Oh fuck," I groaned.

Tucker's eyes twinkled as he grinned.

"Should I just not go?"

"Nope, that'll make it worse. Deal with it. Enjoy the awkward."

Chapter Twenty-One

HARLEY

I didn't know what the hell was going on, but Diego was tense, and Grant was acting weird. As a result, I was anxious. Yoga class, which was my happy place where I was supposed to be able to relax, was freaking tense.

I could feel Diego's gaze boring into me between every posture. He'd practically glared at me when he came in. He always stood in the front. He was the model student now that he and Gemma were all in love and happy.

When Gemma came around to me where I was in my favorite place, way over to the side, I whispered, "What's up with Diego?"

"I wouldn't worry about it," she whispered. "Focus on yourself. Stretch up into my touch." She put the palm of her hand lightly above my fingertips, and I stretched up. "Focus on your body and your breathing," she said softly before moving along.

I tried to follow her advice, but when I glanced over at Grant, he looked worried. A part of me wanted to skip dinner afterward, but it would be obvious because this was a staff night dinner. When dinner was for the guests, some of us cut out and did our own thing. But tonight, it would be noticed if I wasn't there. Plus, the only way I could maybe suss out what was up was to be there.

When I walked into the kitchen, Cat glanced back and forth between Grant and me, giving me a knowing smile. She was savoring the knowledge of her secret a little too much for my comfort. I ignored her and went to the table, sitting between Cammi and Skylar.

Skylar smiled at me. "Hey, hey," I said. "How's it going?"

"Good," Skylar offered.

I glanced at Cammi. "You?"

"Great. I love the website. I need a little help, though," she replied.

"With what?"

"I have more orders than I expected."

"Oh, online orders?" I prompted.

She nodded, her eyes wide. "I thought it would make it easier for my regular customers to be able to order online, but now lots of people are doing it."

"Do you want more online orders?" I asked the obvious.

"Well, yes, but no." She looked flustered.

"Okay, so we could make it so they have to sign up for an account. That's a tiny hurdle. Your regular customers will do that, but it'll weed out others."

"That would be perfect. I want regulars to be able to order ahead, but I'm still adjusting to having Misty Mountain and twins."

Cammi had purchased a second café when the previous owners were leaving, and she was still adjusting to the added business. Not to mention the busyness of twin babies. I chatted casually with her and Skylar about this and that. Diego came over. Once again, I felt his eyes on me. He didn't say anything, so I decided to ignore it.

Skylar looked from Diego to me, her lips twitching. "What?" I asked.

'Nothing," she replied, her tone way too innocent.

"That's not nothing." I countered.

"It sure is," she said forcefully.

I could take a hint and decided to leave it alone. Dinner was tense, at least for me. Undercurrents were flowing between Grant, Diego, me, Skylar, and even Tucker. Although Cat still had her secret knowledge, she seemed out of this little loop. I started to get worried.

———

Cat left after dinner, announcing she had play practice. She was borrowing Nora's truck, meaning Grant and I had the house to ourselves. I fully intended to investigate the tension earlier and took my usual direct approach.

"What the hell is going on?" I asked the minute he came in.

He'd waited a full half an hour after I had left the lodge to come to the staff house, which had me twisted up with impatience inside.

"What do you mean?" he countered as he hung up his jacket and left his shoes by the door.

"Something is up." I stood from the couch, crossing my arms. "Just tell me."

He was quiet for a minute, then took a quick breath. "I talked to Diego."

"What?!" I yelped.

"All I told him was I had feelings for you. I didn't tell him anything had happened."

"Oh my God. I can't believe you did that."

"Harley, I had to say something. You know it'll come down on me if he finds out any other way."

"Well, you didn't have to say anything!" I ground out between gritted teeth.

"Could you just listen? Sit down, please."

"Fine." I plunked on the couch, shimmying back into the corner of the sectional while he sat beside me.

"I do have feelings for you."

"Well, if you had feelings for me, you should've told me, not my brother."

"Would you listen to what I said?"

I tried to take a breath as my heart hammered in my chest. "You have feelings for me?" I repeated.

"Yeah."

"Well, the sex is hot." I tried to divert.

"You know that's not what I mean, and I don't think I'm alone." As I tried to absorb his words, he pressed on, "I didn't expect this, but I don't want to screw this up."

"Why didn't you talk to me before you talked to Diego?"

"Because I don't want this to blow up."

"You don't want to blow this up so you talk to my brother about it?" I countered, my tone sharp.

"All I told him was I had feelings for you. I didn't tell him anything has happened."

"He's not stupid," I muttered.

Grant leaned forward, resting his elbows on his knees and running his hands through his hair. The sound of him taking a deep breath was audible. He lifted his head, his eyes meeting mine. The look there was earnest and intent.

My heart started pounding an echoing drumroll through my body, the crescendo building. So much of what had passed between us since we finally gave in was more than I'd ever expected. Grant wasn't alone. I swallowed, feeling cast adrift on a tide of emotion. The rush of it was enough to sweep me away.

I took another shaky breath. All the while, he watched me quietly. It all felt like too much. Even though I was stubborn and never wanted to back down, I looked away first. I swallowed, my chest feeling tight. My throat was knotted with an unfamiliar emotion.

"Are you okay?" Grant asked.

I heard the rustle of movement, and then he was sitting beside me, sliding his arm around my shoulders.

I shifted, curling into the curve of his shoulder. Grant was everything I didn't want to need, much less want. He was strong, solid, and protective. I didn't need a man to protect me.

I hated how vulnerable I felt with him. Yet that was the tricky part. I hated it, yet I couldn't hide it. I couldn't deny that I trusted him down to my bones.

I would not cry. I would not. Grant, because I sensed he knew I needed not to be pushed, simply held me close with one arm curled around my shoulders.

I pressed my cheek against his chest, the sound of his steady heartbeat soothing me. I finally gathered the courage to lift my head and look him in the eyes again.

"Are you okay?" he repeated.

I nodded. "I'm still annoyed." I mustered enough sass to say that.

His lips twitched at the corners. "I understand. You can be annoyed."

"Of course, I can be annoyed. I *am* annoyed."

"I should have talked to you about it before I said anything to Diego," he said earnestly.

"You should have," I agreed emphatically, lifting my chin.

He angled toward me, lifting a hand to smooth my hair away from my face, his thumb tracing along the edge of my jaw. That subtle touch was like the lick of a flame across the surface of my skin.

"How do I fix it?" he asked.

"Well, you can't unsay whatever you said to Diego. You can rest assured Diego isn't going to forget it."

"I know. Do you want me to talk to him again? I will."

"You already screwed it up," I pointed out.

"Harley, I didn't screw it up."

"It's okay," I said softly.

He went quiet with his eyes studying mine. I felt as if he was peeling away all of my defenses, the armor that had served me so well. Speaking of my defenses, I should have been cranky, *way* crankier than I was about him talking to Diego. Yet the second his lips brushed against mine, I forgot everything.

Chapter Twenty-Two

HARLEY

The following day I had my appointment with Dr. Quinn or Quinn. I couldn't even get his name right. The whole thing made me too anxious.

"So you've had one episode since we met, but it was brief. How are you feeling?" he asked politely.

I shrugged casually. I was determined to downplay this. I could will myself through it. I knew I could.

"I'm fine. I'm ready to start the medication. I thought about it, and you're right. It's not worth the risk." Maybe I was skirting the details, but I *was* willing to listen to him.

Quinn nodded. "It's easy enough to manage. If you do well on the medication, it should minimize your symptoms."

"Will I have this for the rest of my life?"

"Yes."

I sighed. "That sucks. I'm young and healthy."

"On the list of medical issues to deal with, this is very manageable. Diabetes is much more common and causes far more problems."

"I guess I didn't think of it that way."

"It helps to put things in context. We'll start you on a low dose of a beta blocker and see how you do on that. If you have any side effects, let me know right away. We'll try to dial in the right dose to minimize your episodes."

"I'm hoping the lowest dose will work," I said firmly.

He simply nodded, and I thought he was keeping something from me. Being me, I demanded, "Are you trying to hide something from me?"

"No." He chuckled. "You may do well on this dose, but based on your symptom pattern, we'll probably need to increase the dose." I wrinkled my nose and narrowed my eyes. He shrugged. "I'm just being honest."

"I know." I let out a sigh. "Fine."

"Schedule a follow-up on your way out. I'd like to see you in three weeks."

I stood with him, and he held the door for me as I walked into the hallway. He caught me lightly by the elbow just as I was about to turn toward the exit. "Yes?" I prompted.

"Thank you for trusting me and for trying the medication."

"I know you're the expert," I said grudgingly. "I tried it my way, and it didn't work."

"Let's see how it goes. Talk to you in a few weeks."

When I walked out into the waiting area, Diego was there. He stood from a chair when he saw me.

"What are you doing here?" I asked, not even bothering to keep the annoyance out of my tone.

"I saw your car and figured you had an appointment."

"Doesn't my privacy matter here?" I glanced at the receptionist.

She had a headset on and was talking to someone.

My brother rolled his eyes. "I can come in and talk to you."

"Oh, for fuck's sake, Diego. I'm fine. I'm starting the medication." I held up a piece of paper.

"What's that?"

"It's my prescription. Quinn called it into the pharmacy and gave me the printout, which explains my dose and all the small print stuff."

Diego reached for the paper, and I snatched it back, folding it quickly and putting it into my purse. "I will keep you posted."

I walked to the reception desk, took care of my copay, and scheduled my next appointment before we walked out together. He was parked right beside my car.

"You know I love you, right?" He looked down at me.

"I love you too," I muttered. Since this was already a fun, awkward convo, I decided to tackle the next looming topic. "I understand Grant spoke with you."

Diego's brows hitched up. "Oh, he told you he talked to me?"

"He did, and I have one thing to say."

"I'm sure you have something to say," he retorted.

"Stay out of it."

"Does that mean you have feelings for him?" he countered.

I felt heat flash into my cheeks. Diego's brows practically lifted past his forehead. "Wow. I was actually kind of feeling for him. I thought you'd slap him down quick." He cocked his head to the side, looking thoughtful. "Actually, this is probably worse for him."

"What's worse for him?"

"You having feelings for him. If you're even considering this, you have feelings for him."

"Fine," I muttered. "If he hurts me, I'll take care of myself."

"You're my little sister," he said as if that explained everything and gave him some kind of pass to stick his nose into my business. "How would you feel if Gemma hurt me?"

Ah. He had me there. "Fine. Could you just stay out of it?"

"No, I can't. I don't want the details, but Grant talked to me about it, so I can't stay out of it. Plus, I trust him. He told me he was worried about you when you fainted."

I growled in my throat. "Whatever."

Diego held my gaze for a long minute before he stepped closer and pulled me into one of his bear hugs. I squeezed him back, smiling when he stepped away.

"Love you, sis."

"You're supposed to love me. You're my big brother."

He grinned. "I don't have to, though."

Though I was annoyed at him for nosing into my life, my lips twitched with a smile. "I love you too. Now, don't get nosy about Grant and me."

He rolled his eyes, waiting while I climbed in my car and drove away.

Chapter Twenty-Three

HARLEY

The following day, time got away from me. I meant to go over to the lodge for breakfast as the situation in our refrigerator was looking bleak. I had a video conference on a graphic design project, then dived into work, forgetting everything until I went to stand. I was starving and almost light-headed. I stuffed my feet into my shoes and hurried through the trees to the lodge.

Daphne always kept leftovers around. I realized my mistake as I stepped into the back hallway. My heart felt funny, the beats too fast. It felt almost as if my heart stumbled. I saw black dots on the edges of my vision. That was the last thing I remembered until I heard Daphne saying my name. She sounded far away.

"Harley," she repeated.

I blinked my eyes open. She was kneeling beside me, her worried eyes widening the moment mine opened. "Oh, thank God." She sat back on her heels and let out a deep sigh.

"I'm fine," I said.

"Um, you were unconscious."

When she put her hands on her hips and gave me a sort of concerned glare, I almost burst out laughing. Except I felt weak, and, apparently, I'd just fainted in the back hallway at the lodge. Fuck my life.

"I'm fine. It's this heart thing I have."

"I know, you've mentioned it before, but—"

I cut her off. "It's not a big deal. I just started medication for it. My heart skips a beat here and there, and it can get a little out of whack. I need to be careful about not having my blood sugar get low or anything like that. I skipped breakfast this morning. We don't have anything over there. Please don't mention this to anyone."

Daphne studied me quietly. "I sent Cat into town for errands because she has practice tonight for her play. It's just you and me."

She deftly avoided agreeing not to tell anyone. I knew Daphne would say something to Flynn, and Flynn would say something to Diego and Grant. Well, whatever. I resigned myself to the inevitable.

"Should we sit for a minute?" she asked.

"I'm lying flat on my back," I pointed out. She rolled her eyes. "And you're already sitting," I added.

"I am."

Daphne fussed over me, helping me up and herding me into the kitchen, where she sat me down at the table and made me tea. She cooked an omelet, insisting that I needed the protein. I probably did.

She sat with me at the table, nibbling on a leftover scone. "Can I have a scone for dessert?" I asked.

She smiled at me, her eyes twinkling. "Of course. You're another scone lover."

"I like the subtle flavor. They're always a little buttery too." I finished the last bite of my omelet.

She took a sip of coffee before asking, "So how are things with Grant?"

I almost choked on the sip of water I'd just taken. "I'm sorry, what?" I asked after I dabbed the water on my chin with a napkin.

Her lips curled in a knowing smile. "You must know he told Diego he has feelings for you. It's pretty obvious to me that you two have the hots for each other. It's definitely a two-way street. I was just wondering how long it would take. After Cat moved out to the staff house, I figured she would be the unwitting chaperone."

I felt my cheeks heating and ignored it. I mentally sighed and decided to take the honest approach. "Things with us are good."

"Really?" She looked a little surprised I'd shared anything.

"Don't be so surprised. If I'm going to tell anybody, it's you."

"Really?" she repeated, her gaze genuinely curious.

"I trust you. You might mention it to Flynn, but you won't give him the juiciest details."

She laughed softly. "True. So this is a thing?"

"Oh yeah, it's totally a thing. I just didn't want Diego to know it's a thing already. Please don't let Flynn in on that detail."

"I'll keep it vague." She made the cross in front of her heart.

"There was a..." I paused, uncertain what I was trying to explain.

"A spark?" she offered helpfully.

I grinned. "Sure. I thought it would just be a one-time thing, but Grant's a really nice guy."

She nodded firmly. "He's a great guy."

I must have looked distressed because she leaned

over, curling her arm around my shoulders and squeezing quickly. "What's wrong if it's a good thing?" she asked softly as she leaned back.

"I don't know. I'm independent. It's hard for me to rely on anyone. My last boyfriend screwed around on me, but it wasn't like we were in love." I paused, considering the one detail I hated talking about. "When I was sixteen, my sister's boyfriend hit on me. He was twenty-seven."

Her eyes narrowed. "What an asshole and a creep!"

"I told him to fuck off, but I guess it made it hard for me to trust. My sister thought he was the best guy. He was nice and everything."

"What happened?"

"I told her, and she dumped him. It was a big thing. He told her I was lying, but she believed me." Thank God for small favors. My stomach curdled every time I recalled him trying to kiss me after sliding his hand too low past my waist. I'd been horrified. I shook those thoughts away. Sure, it had definitely contributed to my distrust of the world, but it was the past. "Grant doesn't really do serious, does he?"

Daphne was gracious enough to let the conversation move on. "I don't think he's opposed to it. Maybe he hasn't met the right person."

"Yeah, but how can I be the right person? It could get messy."

She shrugged. "We all survived Gabriel and Nora's breakup. You weren't here for the whole of that, but they were pretty cold for a bit there."

"Well, now they're happy. Maybe Grant and I are just meant for a brief thing."

"Do you really like him?" she asked gently.

My heart took off at a fast clip. I took a breath,

letting it out in a sharp sigh. "I think so," I reluctantly admitted. "Has he talked to anybody about it?"

I hated, absolutely hated, my curiosity, but I really wanted to know. If anybody knew, it would be Daphne. "Diego told Flynn that Grant said he had *feeeeeelings* for you. I think you two are good for each other," she offered with a decisive nod.

"Why do you say that?"

"Because you are. Life hasn't been a walk in the park for Grant. Their mom died, and it sounds like their dad was a flake before he passed away. Even with that, Grant's got this easy personality. I think things do come fairly easily to him. You're a challenge for him. He can't just be the guy all the girls want to kiss or fuck, as the case may be," she said bluntly.

I burst out laughing at that. "Are you saying I'm difficult?"

"No. I'm saying you're a challenge for him. You're independent. You're intelligent. You don't need him for anything, and I think that's good for him."

"How is he good for me?"

Her eyes softened. She paused, finishing the last bite of her scone and taking a sip of water before answering. "It seems like you don't trust the universe, especially when it comes to romance. You're kind of prickly." With the way she said it, I couldn't even get defensive, and I snorted a laugh. "Just saying," she offered with a quick grin. "Grant will be good to you, and I think you deserve that."

"Why would he want me? Like you said, I'm prickly."

"I'm kind of prickly."

"No, you're not!" I protested.

Her brows hitched up. "I'm doing better than I

was, but when I met Flynn, I was pretty, well, *really*, uptight. That's why he calls me princess."

I grinned. "I love when he calls you that. It's really sweet."

Her cheeks flushed pink. "I love it too, but it drove me nuts at first. Anyway, sometimes it helps to have someone really good and solid. That's all I'm saying." She paused, her gaze skating over me. "Does he know about your heart issue?"

"Yeah, remember? He's the one who told Diego when I fainted before."

She slapped her hand to her forehead. "That's right!"

"I just started taking medication."

"Will that help?"

"I hope. Quinn said we might have to adjust the dose."

"I think you should let him know this happened."

"I will. I have a follow-up appointment," I said, feeling a little defensive.

"Good. I'd rather not find you passed out in the hallway again. Next time, I'll call Grant or Diego."

I glared at her.

Chapter Twenty-Four

GRANT

A full three days passed before I found out what Harley was hiding.

"I told you about that," Daphne was saying to Flynn in the kitchen at the lodge. "I found her in the hallway. I'd forgotten she has that issue with her heart skipping beats sometimes."

"Found who in the hallway?" I asked just as I stepped into the kitchen.

"Harley. She forgot to eat breakfast and got busy with work. She came over here and fainted in the hallway."

"Is she okay?" I demanded, my tone probably harsher than it should've been. I'd seen Harley every day, so I knew she was fine.

Daphne glanced over. "Yeah, she's fine. Well, you look all tense," she observed as I stopped at the corner of the counter.

"What the hell does that mean?"

Daphne's perceptive gaze skated over me. Her tone was casual when she replied, "Just that. You look tense."

Flynn glanced in my direction, his gaze inscrutable. "We're all a little sensitive about heart stuff," he offered with a glance back at Daphne.

"I know. Harley said she started taking medication."

My blood was beginning to boil. Harley should've told me about this. She hadn't even mentioned that she was taking medication yet. I felt Daphne's gaze on me and tried to school my expression to neutral, but Daphne was annoyingly perceptive. She didn't say anything at that moment, but I saw her eyes narrow slightly and worry chase through her gaze with the telltale furrow between her brows forming. She looked away, replying to something Flynn asked.

Walking to the bathroom in the back hallway, I splashed cold water on my face, quickly drying it with a paper towel and taking a breath. I ordered myself not to dwell on this. I didn't need to worry about Harley. She was fine, right? I didn't need to be angry. It was just that she hadn't told me about this. That tiny detail felt like a splinter driven into the old scar in my heart around my mother's death.

My rational brain tried to remind myself she hadn't known how serious it was until it was too late. I had to splash water on my face again. I took another deep breath, trying to kick all of those worries to the curb.

When I entered the kitchen again, only Daphne was there.

"Where's Cat?" I asked.

"I think she went to town."

I felt unsettled now. I was still hungry, but I didn't want to eat. My stomach was churning.

"I have your favorite," Daphne said.

"My favorite what?" I prompted.

She smiled. "Those ham and cheese rolls you like

so much. I don't know if they're really your favorite, but I know whenever I make them, you gobble them up."

When I rounded the counter, she pushed a small plate in my direction. I picked a roll up and took a bite. It was delicious, but I couldn't even focus.

"Harley didn't tell you," Daphne commented.

"Didn't tell me what?" I asked, though I knew precisely what she was talking about.

Daphne's lips pressed in a line. She placed a rolling pin to the side and quickly rinsed her hands in the sink. While she dried them, she looked over at me. "She doesn't want anyone to worry. I'm worried, and I'm sure you are. I know she means a lot to you."

My heart was making a racket in my chest, and it actually hurt a little. I always thought the whole idea of someone's heart aching was bullshit. But, right now, mine sure did. Tears stung the backs of my eyes, but I wasn't going to fucking cry in front of Daphne. Not because I was being all manly, but because I didn't want her to fuss over me. That would only make it worse.

"You can cry," she said softly.

I blinked, and a single tear rolled down my cheek. I brushed it away. "I don't want to cry. I'm not being all tough."

"I know you're not."

"You know how our mom died," I stated.

She nodded. "This probably brings a lot of shit up."

"Yeah, no shit. I wish Harley would just—" I shook my head. "Fuck. I don't know."

"Talk to her about it. Tell her how you feel."

"For what? She won't even tell me when she has one of her episodes."

"She said she just started taking the medication

and Quinn is going to adjust the dose if needed," Daphne said softly.

I knew she meant to make me feel better, but I felt more annoyed. Harley couldn't even bother to fucking tell me that.

"Well, good," I said, stuffing the rest of the roll in my mouth and taking my anger out on an unsuspecting roll. It tasted like sawdust. It was more just a matter of getting something in my stomach. My stomach was digesting itself with the acid of my anger and confusion about my feelings for Harley.

I knew this was becoming more than just a convenient roommate-with-benefits situation. I didn't get angry often, and that was another splinter in that scar in my heart.

I flew that afternoon, relieved that I had a busy day. Anything to keep my focus off Harley.

That night, I had dinner in town at Sally's.

"Good to see you," Layla said as I walked past her a while later. She cast me a quick smile. The corners of her mouth were tight, and the smile didn't quite reach her eyes.

I wasn't about to explain, but I sensed that she knew our no-strings-on-occasion arrangement was thoroughly over. It was.

I lifted my hand in a wave, tossed a tip on the table, and walked out into the late evening. In most places, it would be dark now, but at this latitude in the summer, even at eleven o'clock at night, the lingering colors from the sunset were still staining the sky. As the indigo darkness came to lay claim, a few stars were already glittering through the colors. A crescent moon sat above the shadowed ridge of the mountains in the distance.

My boots scuffed on the gravel as I crossed the

parking lot. The sounds of the bar became louder before muting as the door swung open and shut again behind me.

I told myself stopping here wasn't a test, but it was. My anger with Harley was still rolling on a low simmering boil inside me. I'd wanted to see if maybe I could feel a spark. But fucking nothing. Nothing. Layla was fun. We always had light, flirty fun. It was easy between the sheets for both of us. Yet Harley had ruined me, likely for all women in the future.

Everything with her was so intense. She'd taken my expectations up another notch. With the way she let her guard down, it felt like I had earned something, something I knew she didn't give over easily.

I drove home. I just hoped Harley and Cat were both asleep. It was almost dark by the time I got back home. I walked from the parking area by the main lodge through the trees to the staff house. My footfalls were quiet on the well-worn ground. An owl called in the distance with an ever-bossy magpie chattering in return.

I stopped as the trees opened up, looking ahead at the small circle of light cast above the porch. I took a breath, squared my shoulders, and walked with purpose.

When I crossed the porch, I knew before I even opened the door that Harley was still awake. Nerves tightened in my gut.

I walked in, calling out, "Hey!"

She was sitting on the couch and glanced over. The silence felt heavy. I left my boots by the door and hung up my jacket. I was just about to cross into the kitchen when her voice stopped me. It was as if she hooked a finger on the back of my shirt and tugged.

"I'm fine."

The anger that had been simmering rolled hot and fast. I spun around. "Why are you hiding things? It's bullshit."

She stood with her hands on her hips. "It's none of your fucking business."

Chapter Twenty-Five

HARLEY

Grant stared at me. My heart was pounding so hard that I felt unsteady for a moment. I reflexively placed my palm on my chest. In a flash, he was at my side.

"Are you okay?"

"I'm fine," I muttered.

Except I wasn't. The pace of my heartbeat felt like a ball rolling down a hill, picking up speed. I sat back down, forcing myself to take several deep breaths. When I opened my eyes, Grant was right there, and my heartbeat was slower.

I lied again, right to his face this time. "I'm fine. I'm just annoyed."

Which was true, except my heart had started to race again.

"Would you tell me if you weren't?" he asked.

"Maybe not. Look, I don't like anybody worrying about me."

Grant was quiet. He felt angry, and Grant never got angry. He was easygoing.

"When people care about you, they worry. Like

Daphne cares. Diego cares. I'm sure your sisters do. We all care."

"I know."

Feeling stubborn, I crossed my arms, twining my forearms together. "Look, it doesn't work for me if you're going to be hovering and worried about everything I do. I don't need to report back when I have an issue. I'm taking medication. It's going to be fine."

Grant closed his eyes. Opening them, he shook his head slowly. "You just don't get it. Why do you have to be so stubborn?"

"Because I am stubborn," I replied, not even caring how mulish I sounded.

"You know, my mom didn't tell us she was having issues until it was too late. For what it's worth, she didn't know until it was too late. You actually know. It really hurts people when they want to help but can't."

He stood and stalked away, sprinting up the stairs. His bedroom door slammed shut.

I was still annoyed, but I also felt twinges of guilt stinging in my heart. I'd be damned if I was going to apologize. I waited until I heard him go into the bathroom and back into his bedroom before I thought about going upstairs. Even after that, I sat quietly in the living room, working on my laptop. Two hours later, I tiptoed upstairs and spent a mostly sleepless night tossing and turning. I finally gave up around four in the morning and powered my laptop on to do more work.

When I heard Grant get up and shower, I thought about going out and telling him I was sorry and that I understood how he felt about his mom. But I was still feeling stubborn and pressed to explain that we weren't the same. I knew what was wrong, and I was taking medication. It would be fine. I didn't need everybody hovering over me.

Chapter Twenty-Six

HARLEY

"You had one episode where you passed out and another when your heart started racing?" Quinn asked.

"Yeah, I was angry," I offered with a shrug.

He arched a brow.

"What? I get angry sometimes. Doesn't everyone?"

"Definitely," he agreed.

"But you strike me as the easygoing type," I said.

The minute I said that, I thought of Grant, who was easygoing. Quinn chuckled.

"Heightened emotions do affect the heart. Are you still going to yoga?"

"Gemma does a class out at the lodge with us. I also usually go once or twice a week in town."

"Good."

"I get that yoga can help me, but how will it help with this?"

Quinn nodded. "Learning to use your breathing to slow down your heart rate is very important. In one of my anatomy classes, a professor said that your lungs and heart are tied together. What one does, the other will follow. You can't consciously bring your heart rate under your control, but you can with your breathing. Use it. It's your friend, and yoga can help with that."

I wrinkled my nose. "if you say so," I teased.

Quinn didn't tease in return. "Getting emotional can affect your pulse. It would be good if you could learn to notice that and slow it down."

"Well, I did sit down, and I breathed," I said, feeling defensive about my breathing and getting angry.

Quinn tapped on a few computer keys. "I'm not saying any of this to be judgmental. Most people get mad. I know you're feeling frustrated that you have to deal with this."

"Well, I am. I'm healthy, and I'm young."

"I can't keep you young, but I can help you stay healthy. I've adjusted the dose. We'll make sure the prescription is sent to the pharmacy. You should be able to pick it up this afternoon."

"Thank you," I forced myself to grind out.

It wasn't Quinn's fault that I sort of blamed him for the situation. But then, I also blamed my last doctor. I was definitely blaming the messenger.

Quinn smiled as I stood. "Please schedule with the receptionist on your way out. I want to see you next month unless something comes up again."

After I left, it felt as if the universe was out to pile on my day. Diego called while I was driving home. I was on autopilot and just tapped the screen on my dash to answer when I saw his name.

"Hey, hey," he said. "Just checking in. I heard from Daphne you had an episode."

"I'm fine," I ground out. "I just left an appointment with Quinn. He's adjusted my medication. I'm fine." I was so freaking sick of everyone worrying about me.

. . .

"I'm your brother. Wouldn't you want to know how I was doing if I had something going on?"

"Yeah, but it's annoying," I replied honestly.

"Well, deal with it. How are things going with Grant?"

"They're not going," I said flatly.

"Hey, you okay?"

"I've had better days." I was feeling crispy on all my edges.

After I got home that evening, under the guise of pretending everything was fine, I had dinner at the lodge. Grant and I did a fantastic job of ignoring each other while conversing with everyone else. It made me tired. I didn't want to admit it, but I missed him.

Only one night without him, and I missed him. The feeling poked at me, little sharp stinging barbs of vulnerability. It was already too much.

I felt so stupid that I'd ever thought this wouldn't get complicated. Fuck my life. It was a big fat mess. The best thing was to stop it in its tracks. We'd have to muddle through this part of it.

I left almost immediately after dinner, claiming I had work to do. The upside to my work was that I could always do something. I hopped online and fiddled around with graphics.

After the third night of Grant and I going through this routine of ignoring each other, I got up in the morning expecting to see him. I didn't want to admit I knew his schedule, but I did. Cat was in the kitchen at the staff house. She took two mornings off from baking, giving Daphne the same in return.

"Hey," she said. She was sitting on the couch with a

cup of coffee in hand and wearing an old pair of sweat-pants with a big fleece top that looked soft and comfy.

"Hey." I went into the kitchen and poured myself a cup of coffee. "Thanks for making coffee," I said as I returned to the living room and took a swallow.

"Sure," she replied. "How come you haven't asked where Grant is?"

"Should I be asking?" I countered.

Cat rolled her eyes. "You two have been doing an excellent job of ignoring the hell out of each other for the past couple of days."

"No, we haven't."

She rolled her eyes. "If you think you two tiptoeing around at night isn't obvious, then you're more naïve than I am."

I felt the heat flash into my cheeks. I took a swallow of coffee to gather my composure before replying, "Whatever. It's not like we're in a rela-tionship."

Cat studied me quietly. "He really likes you."

"I don't think so. He's pissed off because I didn't tell him I had that episode in the hallway. He heard about it from Daphne."

She eyed me over the rim of her coffee mug before draining it and setting it on the coffee table. "You know, sometimes people just worry about each other when they care," she said pointedly. "It's not like I expect you to report to me, but until the past few nights, you've spent every night together."

"I would have told him," I muttered. Defensive-ness grumbled inside.

"You know he's pretty sensitive about health stuff."

"Why?" I pressed even though I knew the answer.

"To this day, I think he feels bad he wasn't here with us when our mom died. He drove home that night, but it was too late. He cares a little bit more than maybe the average person. It might kind of be a thing for him."

I couldn't believe I was getting a lecture from Grant's little sister, and I hated the sharp pangs of guilt I was experiencing. "If it happens again, I'll tell him."

"What's the deal with you all anyway?"

"Well, he's been mad at me about that, so I guess we're taking a break."

"The timing's good, I suppose," she replied.

"What do you mean?"

Her brows hitched up. "Oh, he's gone for two weeks."

It felt as if I was abruptly falling from a great height.

"You didn't know?" she pressed.

"Uh, no. We haven't been talking," I mumbled. I took a quick sip of my coffee, the bitterness matching my mood.

"He's on a two-week tourist-guided trip. Elias was going to do it, but Grant offered when something came up for Elias."

"Oh." I didn't want to even admit how bereft I felt.

"I guess you would have liked to have known, huh?"

I tried to shrug and be nonchalant, but I couldn't even pull it off.

Cat eyed me with sympathy in her gaze. "He'll be gone for two weeks. Maybe that's enough time for you two to sort out your feelings."

"Forced break aside, I see your point. I should have said something. I just, well..." After I stumbled on my words, I blurted out the truth. "I'm still adjusting to having this. I don't like to feel weak."

"I get it. I don't either. I'm the youngest in my family, and everyone else is tough. Even Nora." She rolled her eyes. "Back to Grant. He really likes you. Not like the girls he just has his little nights with."

I didn't even want to think about that. The idea of Grant being with someone else right now elicited a pang of jealousy. I hadn't even felt jealous when I caught my last boyfriend screwing my roommate. I'd been more upset with her than my boyfriend.

"I'll talk to him when he gets back. There's probably no way to reach him."

"Hmm." Cat shrugged. "You'd have to ask Nora if there's a way to radio him. Don't be stupid," she said as she stood. "I like to think you're smarter than me, and here I am lecturing you on your relationship with Grant." She chuckled as she shook her head.

"I appreciate your perspective," I finally managed.

She laughed. "Well, have a good day. I'm hanging out here. If I go over to the lodge, I'll want to help."

"Makes sense. How's your play going?"

"Great."

"When are the performances?"

"Three weeks. I'm super nervous, but I'm also excited."

I grinned. "I think it's cool."

"I've never done anything like this, so I hope it goes okay. Everybody has to start somewhere."

Chapter Twenty-Seven

HARLEY

Everybody has to start somewhere.

Cat's words repeated in my thoughts later on. I had to start somewhere with Grant right now.

Where was I going to start? My mind spun back to when I decided to come up to Alaska.

I didn't want to stay in my apartment because, well, my roommate had been bonking my boyfriend. Just to reiterate, it didn't break me up all that much. It taught me who I couldn't trust. Between that and my older sister's boyfriend hitting on me, well, it was safe to say I was skeptical about romance.

I'd thought with Diego here, it would be fun to visit Alaska. After arriving here and experiencing it—so breathtaking, so beautiful, and welcomed into the family at the resort—I thought I could have a fresh start. I didn't have to have a life that felt defined by who and where I'd lived before.

I sighed as I drove into town that afternoon because, sure, I was in a new location, but I was still the same old me. I was proud of how I'd grown my business and grateful that I could do it anywhere in the world. Yet I couldn't help but wonder if I'd boxed myself in. I told myself I didn't need to overthink this.

I stopped by the grocery store. With Cat at play practice most nights and Grant gone for two whole weeks, I needed some basics. I was making my way through the cracker section when I felt someone stop beside me. Glancing over, I instantly recognized Layla. She happened to look toward me at the same moment and smiled. "Oh, hi."

"Hi," I replied.

Layla was one of the women Grant hooked up with. I had no idea if that had stopped.

"You're Harley, right?" she asked.

I kept a polite smile pinned on my face and nodded. "Yeah. You're Layla, right?"

"I'm friends with Grant," she replied as she nodded. She was quiet for a moment and appeared to be considering her words. "I ran into him just the other day."

"Mmm," I replied vaguely, unsure what else to say.

"He mentioned he was leaving for a two-week trip for work. You work at the resort too, right?"

I nodded again, gritting my teeth because Grant even told *her* he would be out of town. "Yeah, I don't fly the planes, though."

"Oh, cool. I used to be closer to Grant, but I think he's involved with someone." She didn't even seem bothered.

I wanted to scream. More than that, I wanted to be nosy, which I wasn't about to do in the grocery store in front of her. I simply made another vague humming sound and shrugged.

"Grant's a good guy. He should settle down," she said, almost as if she were talking to herself.

"Mmm." That was my go-to in this convo. Blessedly, my phone rang, and I practically snatched it out of my purse. "I need to take this," I said quickly. It was my sister. I didn't have to take it, but it would get me out of this conversation.

"Good to see you," Layla said with a wave before she grabbed a box of crackers and made her way down the aisle.

I stayed put, answering the call. "Hey, Terese."

"Hey, how's it going?"

"Pretty good. Just shopping."

"What's the status?"

"On what?"

My sister's sigh was audible. "You had an appointment with your doctor. You were starting your medication. How's that going?"

"Everything's fine." It was. Quinn said it would be, so I was going with that.

"Diego mentioned you had another episode."

"Oh my God. Is that why you're calling?"

"Yes," my sister retorted sharply.

"It's no big deal. That day I had low blood sugar. I'm fine, okay?"

My sister was quiet before she said, "Okay, I get it. You've always been the tough one."

"What do you mean by that?" Defensiveness sharpened its claws.

"Just that you're the youngest and always need to be tough."

I rolled my eyes even though she couldn't see me. "Whatever. Anything else you need to know?"

I grabbed a box of crackers and began making my way toward the cheese section. "I wanted to check on that and let you know Aunt Sherry passed away."

"Oh no! I'm sorry. I didn't even know she was sick.

Is this a surprise? I saw her just last summer when I went down for a visit."

"I think she was just old," my sister said. "I thought you should know."

"Should I come down for the funeral?"

This was our aunt who didn't have any kids. She was everyone's favorite aunt even though we didn't see her too often because she lived over an hour away from where we'd grown up.

"If you want. I'm going to call Diego after this. I'm guessing he won't be able to make it because I know how busy his flight schedule is in the summer. Let me know if you decide to fly down. We'd love to see you."

"All right. I will. Thanks for calling."

"Love you," she replied.

"Love you more," I returned. We hung up laughing. That was shorthand for us.

After I finished up at the grocery store, I decided to stop by Misty Mountain Café. I didn't like admitting it, but too much time alone wasn't helping me. I considered going to visit my family for my aunt's funeral. I wanted to see them and honor her, and it might get my thoughts off Grant. My brain was looping in circles around him. I told myself I didn't need to be jealous of Layla, but it was kind of ridiculous that he saw her at a fucking bar and told her he would be gone for two weeks. Yet he couldn't bother to tell me. It felt like a betrayal, and I felt childish for even thinking that.

When I walked into the café, it was busy, which was good. Cammi was my friend, and I wanted her to be busy. I was glad to see she was working the counter. She flew through the orders for the customers ahead of me. It was only a few minutes before I was at the register.

"Hey!" she said with a bright smile.

"Hey, I figured I could grab an afternoon coffee."

"You should go to yoga class tonight," she suggested.

"I should?"

"Gemma's doing a new heated yoga class. I can't wait."

"Oh. I've heard of that. I've never done it, though."

"I love sweating," Cammi said. "Maybe because I've grown up in Alaska and even the summers here aren't that hot."

I chuckled. I ordered, waiting while Cammi prepped my coffee. "So you must be on your own at the staff house then with Cat busy with the play and Grant gone for two weeks."

I paused. "How do you know about Grant being gone?" I asked.

"He mentioned he would be gone on one of those longer trips," she said slowly. "Elias mentioned it too."

I felt my nostrils flare when I took a breath. "Everybody knew but me," I finally blurted out.

"Are things okay with you two?"

"We had an argument. It's no big deal. I think it's for the best."

"What's for the best? That you had a fight?"

I rolled my eyes. "No, that Grant's gone for two weeks. He couldn't even bother to tell me. I think that's sort of like a roommate respect thing."

Cammi studied me quietly. "Hang on." She passed my coffee over the counter and spun around, pushing through the swinging door into the back. A moment later, a teenage girl came out, dusting her hands on her apron and rinsing her hands in the sink. She turned and smiled at me expectantly. "Can I help you?"

"Oh, I've already got mine."

Cammi appeared behind her. "Come in the back. Let's chat."

"The back?"

"Yeah, I own the place." She gestured for me to come behind the counter.

I slipped through the opening when she lifted a portion of the counter where it was hinged and followed her into the back where I'd never been. My gaze arced around the space. Even back here, it was cheerful and warm. There was a wide stainless-steel table in the middle of the room.

"What are you making today?" I asked.

"Oh, I do all the prep in the morning. Sit." She patted a stool.

Once I was seated, she sat on a stool beside me. She took a swallow from a mug on the table. Setting it down, she commented, "I needed a break. You want some pizza?"

Before I could reply, she hurried over to one of the ovens and peered inside. "I'm making mini pizzas."

"I love pizza. It's a balanced meal," I teased. She grinned and slid out a pizza. "Ooh, is that pepperoni?"

"Yup, I've got this and a few veggie options."

A few minutes later, I glanced over. "Cammi, everything you make is good."

Her blue eyes twinkled with her smile. "What's up? You're upset because Grant hadn't mentioned he was going out of town."

I finished chewing. "It would've been nice to know."

"What was the argument about?"

I sighed, knowing I'd have to explain. "I have this heart thing." I quickly summarized, ending with, "It's not a big deal. Totally treatable. Anyway, he got mad at me because he thought I was covering it up. I just learned from Cat the other night that health things are a sore spot for him."

Cammi nodded sagely. "Because their mom died from an undiagnosed condition. I think he feels bad because he was off at college in Anchorage."

"That's not his fault," I protested.

"Well, of course not," she said, lifting a hand and letting it fall. "But grief doesn't always make sense. Grief is emotional, old patterns, and all that. Logic doesn't play into it. Elias thinks Grant really likes you."

"How would he know?"

"Elias is pretty perceptive. He's quiet but dangerous."

"Dangerous?"

She giggled. "He's a softy, but he picks up on what's going on. Apparently, the guys had drinks at Sally's the other night, and one of Grant's usual pickups wasn't getting anywhere even though she tried." I shouldn't have felt a little thrill at that, but I did. "How do you feel about him?"

I finished off a slice of pizza. After swallowing, I shrugged. "I didn't think I would really fall for him. I thought we would have a little fun, and that would be that."

"What's your history with relationships?" she asked.

"Huh?"

"You know what I mean. I was burnt like a crispy marshmallow when I met Elias. But if it's the right person, you can get past it."

"I don't know. The last guy I was dating screwed around with my roommate. Before that, my older sister's boyfriend hit on me when I was sixteen. He was over ten years older," I offered with a grimace.

Cammi's eyes widened. "Look, that was creepy, but my sister dumped him, and I wasn't heartbroken about my ex. In short, though, I learned who I couldn't trust."

"Them," she offered succinctly. "You seem like a person who doesn't let your guard down easily."

I instantly felt prickly inside even though I knew she had a point. "What do you mean?"

"We're all different people, and we all have different experiences. You seem very independent. I don't mean that in a bad way. The world is a hard place for women to live. That alone is enough for a woman to be guarded, and that doesn't take into account assholes like your ex or creeps like your sister's ex."

I thought maybe it was just that. Layered into the mix with me being the youngest in my family, I'd felt like I spent my childhood fighting to show that I was tough, not the one who everybody told what to do. It's possible, just a little bit, that I was stubborn and hated everyone always babying me.

I realized Cammi was waiting for me to say something. "I suppose I am independent."

"When it's right, it feels right. And this might seem weird, but when it's right, it's also scary."

"What do you mean?" My pulse kicked up a notch.

"Not scary in a bad way. Because it matters. It's one thing to like someone and have it not work out. It's another thing to love someone."

I knew precisely what she meant. What happened with the last guy I dated had stung my pride, but it didn't break my heart.

"Grant's one of the good guys."

"I know." I sighed. "I wish he'd told me he would be out of town."

"Did you give him a chance to tell you?"

Her question felt barbed even though I knew she

didn't intend that. I felt heat rise in my cheeks. "Maybe not," I muttered.

Cammi smiled warmly, reaching over and squeezing my shoulder. "He'll be back, and you can talk then."

Someone called her name from the front. "I should probably get back out there."

"You should. Thank you," I said as we stood together.

"For what?"

"For being my friend." She smiled and gave me a quick hug.

As I drove toward the lodge, I decided I might as well go to my aunt's funeral. Grant was gone, so I would just be twiddling my thumbs.

Chapter Twenty-Eight

GRANT

I leaned on the railing of the walkway, the sound of rushing water filling the air. I had flown a group out to Brooks Falls in Katmai National Park & Preserve. This area became famous due to the live video showing the massive brown bears who fed on the salmon here. Of course, it was also a place of breathtaking beauty. I'd seen my fair share of bears and preferred to stay at a comfortable distance at all times.

"Hey, Grant," a feminine voice reached me.

I turned to see Lacey Haynes approaching. "Hey, Lacey, what are you doing out here?" I asked.

"What do you think I'm doing out here?" she countered when she stopped beside me.

I smiled at her. Lacey was a kick-ass wilderness guide and married to Quinn Haynes. "I thought you were pregnant," I commented.

"I am," she replied with a grin. "But I can still hike. This is my last trip before I stay put in Diamond Creek." With her auburn hair and sparkling green eyes, Lacey had an earthy beauty to her. "How long are you here?" she asked.

"Oh, I've got a whole tour group. We're stopping here for a night, and then I'm flying them to another stop. They're fishing and doing all the things, so a few more puddle jumpers." Puddle jumper flights in Alaska were the short flights people took all over the wilderness since most of the state was only accessible by boat or plane.

"Flying over here isn't really a puddle," she offered.

I chuckled. "True."

She rested her elbows on the railing, and we watched a brown bear snatch a salmon in its jaws.

"So how are you and Harley?"

Lacey's question startled me. "Excuse me?"

"Aren't you two a thing?" She waved her hand in the air.

"What do you mean 'a thing'?"

"Oh my God, Grant. I think you know what I mean."

I pressed my tongue into my cheek as I shook my head. "Okay, fine. I guess we were involved. Then we had an argument. I'm not really sure what our status is right now," I answered honestly.

"What was the argument about?"

"Are you always this nosy?" I asked.

"Grant, we're in the middle of freaking nowhere. The group I brought over is out hiking for the day, and I'm just here killing time. We might as well discuss something juicy."

I chuckled. "Fair enough. Well, she's got this heart problem, and she hasn't really kept me up to speed. It's possible I overreacted."

"It's possible? That means you overreacted," she deadpanned.

I bit back a sigh.

"Is it because of your mom?" Lacey grew up in Diamond Creek, so she knew my family's history.

"Maybe I worry about medical stuff more than the average person."

"Yeah. Like Quinn."

"Uh, he's a doctor," I pointed out dryly.

"Not like that. I have MS, so he worries extra about me. Your mom died of a heart condition that nobody knew she had, so you worry a little extra about people you love. Once something like that happens, it's kind of a thing."

I stared out over the river, watching as a bear leaned down and snatched a salmon out of the water, eating it right there by the shore. "I guess you have a point," I finally said.

"Does Harley know that?"

"Yeah, I think so."

"She's independent." Lacey offered.

"How well do you know her?" I returned.

She shrugged. "Takes one to know one."

I chuckled. "Ah, I see."

"Quinn and I have been together for years. He's still not happy with my job choice."

"Didn't he used to do guiding trips with you?"

"He still does here and there, but he prefers for me to stay close to home. I don't always do that, and he's learned to live with it. We have a plan for emergencies, and my MS is under control. But I get it. Some of us just have that streak, and the people who love us have to deal with it."

The minute she said that, my heart lunged in my chest, kicking up a racket against my ribs.

"You have a reaction to the idea of love, huh?" she pressed.

"Oh, for fuck's sake, Lacey."

She grinned. "It seems like Harley means something to you. No judgment, but you don't really do relationships. Not that I know of." I stayed quiet, but I knew she had a point. I didn't for a long time because I had other priorities. "It's just a vibe, but I think you and Harley might be a good thing," she added.

"You think?"

"Yeah. You're not going to get scared away by an independent woman." She nodded firmly in emphasis with that.

Harley exuded a sense of independence, of boldness, as if she dared anyone to question her. I thought back to the very first night I kissed her after she chased off a moose with a shovel and a rock.

"No, that doesn't scare me off," I agreed.

"So tell Harley how you feel," Lacey pressed.

"I can't exactly do that right now. Communication isn't that convenient here."

"As soon as you get back then."

I absorbed that. "This was an unexpected conversation," I finally said.

"Deep moments with Lacey Haynes in the wilderness," she offered dryly.

I burst out laughing at that. "Fair enough. When's the baby due?"

"Five months. Like I said, Quinn and I have to compromise sometimes. I told him this was my last trip, so I'll stick to it. I do lots locally, though. I do mostly management these days. I don't lead many hikes myself, but I like seeing places."

"You've been here. Lots," I pointed out.

"I know, and I love it. Every time I look at that..." She gestured toward the river. A brown bear was in the falls, and two were along the river's shore. She lifted her hand higher, gesturing to the mountain ridge in the distance. "It's Alaska. It never fails to take my breath away."

"I know."

We smiled at each other. A moment later, a raven flew past, the sound of its wings swishing through the air.

Chapter Twenty-Nine

GRANT

I thought about Lacey's advice a week later. I'd had plenty of time to think. I missed Harley—a lot—and I knew I loved her. I just had to tell her.

The trip was going smoothly with the weather on our side. We were spending the last stop in Kodiak. There were brown bears, and then there were Kodiak brown bears. Kodiak brown bears were a unique subset. As one of the largest bears in the world, they had been isolated from other bears on the islands of the Kodiak archipelago for over 12,000 years. There was no other way to put it—they were fucking huge.

After we landed in Kodiak, I got the group set up at a local B&B in town, checked into my room, and then headed out for dinner. One of the perks of flying all over Southcentral Alaska was I had friends all over. Alaska was a big state geographically, but the way of life here tied its residents together. I didn't have to see the bartender at the local hangout very often for us to be buddies. The owner at the B&B knew me well. Nana felt like a grandmother to me even though I'd only seen her maybe once or twice a year in all the years I'd been flying. She always reached up and patted me on the head, which cracked me up.

"All right, now don't be late." As if to remind me, she stretched up and patted me on the head.

I grinned down at her. She insisted on everyone calling her Nana. I didn't know if she had another name.

"I won't be late. I have an early flight out tomorrow."

"Be careful walking into town. We've had some bear activity lately. Just so you know."

"I'm always careful," I replied.

It was a ten-minute walk into town. I had dinner and was walking back when I heard a human scream nearby. I picked up to a jog, fetching the bear spray I kept tucked in my cargo pants.

On the heels of another scream, I came around the corner on the road. It was dusk, but I could see two bear cubs perched on a small rise and the mama bear standing over a man curled up on the ground on the side of the road.

"Shit," I muttered to myself.

Shifting, I pulled my sidearm out of its harness. I glanced around to make sure no one was nearby before firing it straight up into the air. The mama bear turned her attention to me, approaching quickly. Bears were big and lumbering, but damn, they could cover some fucking ground.

I let loose with the bear spray, preferring not to shoot her because she had two cubs, and they needed her. She stopped at a distance, but then she started toward me again. I got a shot off, but it missed her. She sideswiped me in the leg with her claws, the bear's equivalent of a cat batting at a toy. To my relief, she bolted after that with her cubs right behind her.

My thigh burned like hell. I limped over to the man, keeping my eyes on the bear's path. She and her cubs beat feet into the trees.

"You okay?" I asked when I reached the man.

He slowly uncurled and sat on the ground. I saw the blood running down his shoulder.

"She just came out of the trees," he muttered, appearing disoriented and in pain.

I yanked my phone out. Thank God we were within cell range here. I'd been contemplating calling Harley ever since we landed. Instead, I was calling the emergency services and waiting with this guy on the side of the road.

An hour or so later, I was at the reception desk in the emergency room. "Now, can you remind me of your insurance number again?"

I glanced at the woman behind the desk. "Look, I don't fucking know, and I don't have my card on me. Hang on, let me call my office."

A moment later, I was holding my cell phone to my ear as I listened to the phone ring. I started to think perhaps Daphne wasn't there, but she answered, "Hello?"

Relief whooshed through me. "Hey, Daphne. It's Grant."

"Hey, why are you calling?"

"Well, I'm in Kodiak, which is a damn good thing because I'm at the hospital."

"What?!" she yelped.

"I'm fine. I got swiped by a bear on my leg. I'm all stitched up, but I can't find my insurance card."

"Are you sure you're okay?" she demanded.

"It hurts like hell, but yeah, I'm fine." The receptionist's eyes widened. I shrugged. "I'm gonna hand the phone over to this nice woman who's trying to give me my discharge paperwork."

"Grant, I have lots more questions," Daphne warned.

"I know, but first things first." I glanced at the woman's name tag. "This is Linda. Here you go." I smiled at Linda, adding, "Linda, this is Daphne on the other end of the phone." I handed it over.

Linda asked Daphne a few questions while she rapidly typed away on her computer.

"I'm back," I said into the phone a few moments later.

"Grant! You scared me," Daphne announced.

"I'm fine."

"Are you in a hospital bed?"

"No, I'm checking out. I'm just limping."

"What the hell happened?"

"Fortunately, Nana at the B&B where I am staying, gave me a heads-up that there have been a few bear sightings in town, so I had my bear spray and my gun. I didn't get the worst of it. A guy was walking ahead of me before I saw him and startled a mama brown bear with two cubs. She tore open his shoulder, and he'll be dealing with that for a long time. I got some bear spray off and one shot. She swiped me on the leg when she ran by, and then she took off."

"Grant!"

"What? I'm fine. I swear." I still had some residual adrenaline from the altercation. My leg throbbed, though. "They cleaned me up and stitched up the deeper gash," I explained.

"Jesus," Daphne muttered. "I know there are bears here, and I've seen some from a distance, but I don't like thinking about this." She sniffled.

"Are you crying?"

"Yes. I care about you. You're family to me," she replied, her voice watery.

I stopped joking about it. "Hey, Daphne, I'm really okay. I was going to call as soon as I was done with the hospital, but I couldn't find my insurance card, so I had to call sooner. Where's Flynn?"

"I don't know." She sniffled. "He's having dinner with the guys in town."

"Okay. Have him give me a call when he gets there. I promise I'm okay. I can have the doctor call you."

"No, I believe you. Y'all aren't allowed to scare me like this."

"Hey, I wasn't trying to scare you."

"Well, you did," she said stoutly. "Do I have your permission to tell everyone?"

"Tell everyone you want. Make it sound worse than it was, so people will think I'm a total badass. I chased the bear off, saved the other guy, and just got a little scratch for all my trouble. It's a souvenir, you know," I teased.

"Oh my God, you are ridiculous. I can't believe you're making light of this."

"This reminds me. You carry bear spray when you're on your own, right?"

"Of course, I do. Flynn won't let me go anywhere without it."

"I think we need to plan some shooting lessons."

"What?" she squeaked.

"Yes, it's time for Cat to learn more about handling a gun, so you might as well learn too. It'll be helpful if we ever end up with a bear that lingers nearby. You don't have to carry the gun everywhere you go, but you need it nearby."

"Grant, this isn't making me feel better," she warned.

"We'll talk about it when I get back. Can you do me a favor?"

"Of course, you know I'll do anything you ask."

"Give Harley or Diego a call. Let them know what's going on."

"Harley's out of town."

My stomach flipped. "What?"

Daphne let out a soft sigh. "Their aunt died. She and Diego went down for the funeral, but he's already back."

"Do you know when she'll be back?"

"No. Diego just said she decided to stay a little longer. I know you're in love with her, but why do you care?" she asked pointedly.

Daphne had opinions about her friends' relationships. I could practically see her lifting her chin and narrowing her eyes at me. "What do you mean why do I care? Of course, I care."

I ignored the part where she said I was in love with Harley. I *was* in love with Harley, but I wasn't ready to talk about it.

"Because you left for weeks without letting her know you were going to be gone."

I gritted my teeth, my breath hissing through them. "You know I meant to tell her."

"Bullshit. You purposely didn't tell her. Come on. Everybody else knew except Harley, and you're roommates."

"I know we're roommates," I ground out, my jaw still clenched.

"I will call her for you. In the meantime, I suggest you think about how you feel."

I felt like a child being scolded by a teacher. "Jesus, Daphne, I just got attacked by a bear."

"Oh, all of a sudden, it's a big deal. You just told me it was no big deal."

She had me there. "Fine, fine."

"Why don't you call her? Apparently, you have cell reception," she pointed out.

I took a breath. "I do. I will try to call her, but it's spotty here, you know?'

"Oh, is it? It sounds crystal clear. You could call her right this second."

"I might try."

"I'll still call her just so she's up to speed. Now, when will you be home?"

"Well, the schedule is for me to fly back in two days."

"But you got attacked by a bear."

"Yeah, and I'm stitched up. I'm limping, but I can still fly."

"Are you freaking serious?"

"Yeah, completely."

"Ugh," she muttered. "Sometimes there are too many tough guys around here."

I chuckled. "Love you, Daph. See you when I get back."

I stared down at the phone. My heart started pounding, a roll of thunder reverberating through my body.

Daphne was exactly right. I had intentionally avoided telling Harley I'd be out of town. I just hadn't wanted to tell her I would be gone. I loved her. Fuck.

I tapped open my texts, finding our last exchange and hitting the call icon. I didn't need to be a chicken about this. Not anymore.

I was so nervous my pulse was racing. When her voicemail picked up, I thought it was her answering for a split second, and my breath seized. "Hey, it's Harley. You know what to do."

At the click, I hesitated for a long second before saying, "Hey, Harley. It's Grant. I'm sorry about your aunt. I'd like to talk to you soon."

My lips literally vibrated with the urge to tell her I loved her, but I wasn't sure we were there yet. I hung up, feeling foolish. When I looked back down at the phone, I almost called again, but I didn't.

Chapter Thirty

HARLEY

I played Grant's message once again, holding my breath during his long hesitation at the end, and wondered what he was thinking. My stomach felt hollow, and my heart pounded with nervous anticipation.

I missed him so much that my heart throbbed with a dull ache.

As I was staring at the screen, my phone vibrated in my hand again. I glanced down to see Daphne's name flashing.

"Weird," I said aloud as I slid my thumb across the screen to answer. "Hey, what's up?"

"Hey, it's Daphne."

"I know," I pointed out.

"Oh."

Her pause was a little longer than expected. "I assume you're calling for a reason," I prompted.

"Um..." she began before pausing again.

"Daphne, what the hell is going on?"

"Everything's fine. Grant asked me to tell you that."

"He asked you to call me and tell me everything's fine?"

"Well, he got attacked by a bear."

"What?!" I screeched.

"Yeah, that's pretty much what I said," she said calmly. "We haven't seen him yet. He's in Kodiak. All we know is he was walking back to the B&B where he is staying, and somebody ahead of him startled a mama bear. He sprayed bear spray, got a shot off, and she swiped him on the leg."

"Oh my God," I breathed.

I vividly remembered the size of the claws I'd seen on the stuffed brown bears on display at the Anchorage airport, of all places. I remembered saying to Diego while we were waiting for our flight that that was as close as I ever wanted to get to one of those bears.

"Are you sure he's okay? Can somebody fly to go get him?"

"Flynn's already talked to him, and Flynn thinks it's fine. I'm with you. I feel like somebody should go get him. Grant says he's fine, and the doctor says he's fine. I don't know. He asked me to call you. I'm curious, though."

"About what?"

"It's kind of nosy, so is it okay if I ask?"

I sighed. "Daphne, you're always nosy."

"So are you," she countered.

I was too worried about Grant right now to care. "What's up?"

"Did he call you?"

"Yeah, he left me a message. He didn't mention he got attacked by a bear," I said dryly.

"Maybe he didn't want to leave it on a message. I told him to call you, so I'm glad he did."

"Are you sure he's okay?" I repeated.

"I've told you everything I know. I'd recommend you call him back. When Flynn spoke to him, he was still at the hospital waiting to be cleared for discharge. He let one of the nurses talk to Flynn, and she assured Flynn that he was okay. She said he'll probably be sore. He's got some stitches to get taken out when he's back."

"Oh God," I breathed. She simply repeated what she'd already shared, but my emotions were cresting. My throat ached with unshed tears, and I tried to take a breath.

"Are you okay?" Daphne asked.

I was most definitely *not* okay.

"You know Grant's in love with you, don't you?"

"How do you know that? Is that what he said?" I demanded.

"I just know. How do you feel about him?"

"I don't know," I burst out.

"Maybe you should come home so you can talk to him face-to-face. When will you be back?"

"I scheduled my return ticket in three days. I haven't been gone that long," I replied defensively.

"I wasn't implying you had," she said gently. "Get back as soon as you can. Stay safe."

"Okay." Just as I was about to hang up, I prompted, "Daphne?"

"Yeah?"

"Thank you for calling me."

"Of course. Miss you, girl. We'll see you when you get back."

Chapter Thirty-One

HARLEY

"How do you think you feel?" Terese, my oldest sister, asked.

I narrowed my eyes. "If I knew how I felt, I wouldn't be asking you."

My sister pursed her lips, her brows hitching up. "Hmm. I think you know how you feel. You're just avoiding it. Just like you avoided this thing with your heart."

"I did *not* avoid it," I muttered.

She cocked her head to the side. "Really? How come you didn't mention it to any of us when you knew while you were still living down here?"

"Because it's not that big of a deal."

She studied me quietly before leaning forward and resting her elbows on the table. "You know, sometimes I complain about being the oldest, but I've always thought it's got to be the worst to be you."

"What do you mean?"

"Lord knows, we have many blessings in our family. Our parents loved each other. They loved us. We love each other. Oh, we've been through some shit, but so has every family. We're all pretty outspoken. Being the youngest, I imagine it's always felt like you had to fight to be heard."

I laughed softly. "Sometimes I feel like nobody listens to me."

"When we were little, you always tried to prove that you were as fast as us, as smart as us, as tough as Diego."

My eyes stung with tears as I cast her a rueful smile. "I suppose so, but what's so bad about that?"

"Well, it's a hard thing. Nobody wants to deal with a health issue when they're young. And you *definitely* don't like any of us worrying about you."

"No, that drives me crazy."

"We love you, so we get to worry."

"I know, and I love you too." My throat was tight, and my chest felt itchy with heat.

"Would you want me to hide something like that?" Terese asked gently.

"No," I retorted, taken aback.

"Exactly."

"What does this have to do with Grant?" I asked.

"It's your heart," she began. I rolled my eyes. "My point is you like being in control, and falling in love is something you can't really control."

"I don't—"

I started to argue, but my sister's brows hitched up, her lips kicking up at one corner in a knowing smile. "Don't you? We all do to an extent. I'm just saying the need for control runs strong with you."

I snorted. "I suppose."

"Get your ass on that plane and go back early. You're freaking out because he got attacked by a bear, which sounds like a joke."

"There are bears in Texas too," I pointed out.

"I know, but we don't have those big-ass ones in Texas," she returned.

"I'll text Diego. He can pick you up at the airport," she offered.

"No need. My car's there, so I'll drive myself back. Plus, don't tell Diego."

"Why?"

"Because I want to surprise Grant. If Diego knows, he'll tell somebody, and keeping it a secret will be impossible."

"Okay. Just for practice, tell me how you feel about Grant." My sister's gaze was soft with understanding.

With emotion rushing through me, I took a deep breath. "I love him."

"You said it!" she whisper-shouted.

"Oh my God," I murmured.

"When it really matters, it's not that easy to say."

Chapter Thirty-Two

HARLEY

Even though I moved my flight up, I still had to wait another day. I was impatient every minute. I texted Daphne repeatedly, checking to see if anything had changed with Grant. She assured me she had spoken to him more than once and that he was okay. I didn't even tell her I was coming back early. I'd booked the first leg of my flight as a red-eye during the night so I could sleep. Except I could *never* sleep on a plane. I envied the people who could.

By the time Anchorage came into view late the following afternoon, I was cranky and tired as our plane descended to land. The view was breathtaking, with the afternoon sun bathing the mountains in shades of gold and silver.

I was nervous just getting here. It would be hours yet until I could see Grant because now I had a drive ahead of me. While my car was at the airport, I was now doubting the wisdom of my plan because I was exhausted. But I was also stubborn, and I wasn't going to delay. I hopped in my car and started driving. The last thing I remembered was the crunch of metal and a jarring impact.

My eyes flew open, and the sound of my scream ricocheted around me.

Chapter Thirty-Three

GRANT

Flynn grinned as he approached me inside the plane hangar. As soon as he stopped in front of me, he pulled me into a back-slapping hug. Stepping back, he offered, "You look okay. You must have showered this morning."

I chuckled. "I did. I was staying at Nana's place. She has plenty of hot water."

Whenever we booked these longer trips, we often flew into less developed areas. As a result, hot showers and good food weren't always an option. I didn't mind that, but it was nice to end in a place where I could enjoy the amenities.

"How're you doing? How's your leg?" he asked, glancing down. "Can't see a thing, man."

I chuckled. "There's a tidy row of stitches on my thigh. Not too bad, but it hurts like hell," I said honestly.

"How bad is it?"

"Oh, she got me good. Only one of the gashes needed stitches though. The doctor said getting the area clean was more important than the stitches. They were concerned about the other guy. He was in much worse shape."

"Yeah?"

"He'll be dealing with an achy shoulder for the rest of his life. He has a few torn ligaments."

"Oh man, I bet he's glad you came along," Flynn commented.

"I'm just glad Nana mentioned there'd been some bears around. I don't always carry my gun and bear spray when walking through town."

Flynn shook his head slowly. "No shit, neither do I."

He helped me take care of the plane before we closed up the hangar and walked out.

"How was the trip overall?"

"Pretty good. Except for the bear."

My elder brother gave me a long look before pulling me into another big hug. My throat was tight when he stepped back. "You gave us a scare."

My voice was rough as I replied, "Didn't mean to. I'm all in one piece, I swear."

———

That evening at dinner, I missed Harley's presence at the table. After the guests filtered out of the kitchen, it was just me, Flynn, Daphne, Nora, and Gabriel hanging out. Cat was at her play practice.

"Beer?" Gabriel prompted as he held one aloft.

I shook my head. "Nah, kind of tired."

"Suit yourself," he replied as he sat down at the table.

"When do you get your stitches out?" Nora asked.

"They said two weeks. The nurse at the hospital in

Kodiak already scheduled a follow-up with Quinn. He'll take care of it."

"You're damn lucky, you know?" Gabriel prompted.

"I know. Honestly, I don't normally walk around town with my gun and bear spray, but Nana mentioned there'd been bear sightings, so I did it to be safe. Thank God."

Daphne slid a look at Flynn. "I didn't mention it, but Grant thinks I need shooting practice."

Flynn nodded. "You do."

Daphne's eyes went wide, her mouth falling open slightly. "Are you serious? I don't think that's necessary. I have my bear spray."

"Bear spray helps, but it would be good for you to feel comfortable with gun basics. We live out here where bears are even more likely," Flynn countered.

"I know, but they keep their distance," Daphne insisted.

"They usually do. But look, it's been years..." He glanced at me. "Remember that summer?"

"Oh yes."

"What summer?" Daphne asked.

Nora grinned. "We had a problem with a male brown bear one summer. He kept lingering. It was my fault because I left the trash out one night. Anyway, we had to keep a gun right by the door in case he showed up so we could get to it quick."

Daphne's eyes widened.

"He eventually left, but it was a nuisance for a while," Flynn said.

"Fine," Daphne said, her tone resigned.

"Dinner was great," I said, catching Daphne's eyes.

She smiled. "Thank you. I made one of your favorites."

"Mac and cheese is always my favorite. You can make it every night," I replied.

"I'm not going to make it every night. The guests wouldn't appreciate it."

"Oh, I think they would," Gabriel chimed in.

We all laughed. Just then, the main phone to the lodge rang. An old phone was mounted on the wall by the door into the back hallway, but it was rarely used. We collectively swiveled, looking in that direction.

Daphne commented, "I'll let it go to voicemail."

"Do you have the volume turned up?" Flynn asked.

"I don't know." Daphne hurried across the kitchen. "Oh yeah, it's on."

A moment later, we heard the lodge message in Daphne's polite voice with a subtle Southern twang, followed by, "Hello, this is Jen Williams from the Emergency Response Team in Diamond Creek. Please give me a call as soon as you can."

"What the hell?" Flynn muttered.

Daphne was calling the number on her cell phone as it was recited in the voicemail. A moment later, she was saying, "Hello, I'm calling from Walker Adventures. You just left us a message." She nodded along while we all waited. "Oh, right. I can get you her brother's phone number. Hang on." She gestured to Flynn, adding, "It's about Harley. Something happened. Write down Diego's number for me. I don't have it memorized."

"What happened to Harley?" I practically barked as Flynn jotted down Diego's number on a napkin.

Daphne held a finger up. "Yes, yes. Can you tell us where she is? Yes. Okay, thank you. We'll be in touch."

"What the hell is going on?" I asked, standing from the table. I was jolted out of my relaxed state.

"Harley was in an accident," Daphne explained.

"Is she okay?" My heart was pounding erratically.

"She's at the hospital."

"Which hospital?" I demanded.

"The officer said she was between Diamond Creek and Kenai but closer to Diamond Creek, so that's where they took her."

"We have to go." I was already walking toward the back hallway.

"He said she's okay. They're not sure what caused the accident. It was a single-car accident. She ran into the guardrail, and her car bounced to the other side. They need to call Diego because he's her closest family," Daphne explained.

I kept walking across the kitchen with Flynn calling, "I'm coming with you. I don't want you driving."

Moments later, Flynn and Daphne were in the front seat of the lodge SUV while I was in the back. Nora and Gabriel stayed at the lodge in case there were any calls.

"What the hell could have happened? She wasn't even supposed to be back for two more days," Daphne said. "Did you ever talk to her?"

"Ah, no. I left her a message the day before yesterday, and she hadn't called back."

"The woman who called said she was okay. Oh my God. I hate waiting." Daphne's phone rang, and she answered it. "It's Diego," she offered over her shoulder. "Hey, Diego, did they give you more information than me?"

I wanted to snatch the phone from her hands. She was nodding along. "Yes, we're on our way. Yeah? Okay." A moment that felt like forever stretched before she hung up. "He doesn't know what caused the accident. He got more information from the hospital. She was knocked out, but she's conscious now, and it doesn't appear anything's broken. She has a cut on her shoulder from broken glass."

I leaned my elbows on my knees, trying to take slow breaths.

"You okay back there?" Flynn called over his shoulder.

"Yeah, I'm all right," I lied.

The rest of the ride was quiet. For every minute of it, I regretted that I hadn't told Harley I loved her yet. I'd been stupid and childish after she got upset with me for talking to Diego. It had been petty to just take off on this trip. One of the other guys would have done it. Maybe she wouldn't have had this accident if I'd been here. Maybe, maybe, maybe. All I knew was I needed to see her. The urge was so powerful I felt like I was going to jump out of my skin.

It felt like forever before we got to the hospital. Daphne and I raced inside while Flynn parked.

"We're here for Harley Jackson. We're family," Daphne said as soon as we got to the reception desk.

The woman there glanced down, tapping on her keyboard. "She's just been brought in. She's in an examination room right now. I'll tell the doctor you're here. As soon as they have an update, someone will come out to speak with you."

"Can you tell me how she is now?" I burst out.

The woman looked up, her gaze calm. "She was stable when she arrived."

"Is that all they can tell us?" I muttered a few minutes later as we sat in the waiting area.

"That's probably all she knows," Daphne said, patting my arm.

I was determined to tell Harley how I felt. It didn't matter anymore if she wasn't ready yet. I had faith she would be.

Chapter Thirty-Four

HARLEY

My shoulder throbbed.

"How are you feeling?" the nurse asked.

My eyes dipped down to her name tag, which said Helen. She had a very practical air to her. Her hair was twisted into a braid, and her blue eyes were kind.

"I'm confused," I finally said.

She smiled softly. "Do you remember what happened?"

"I think I fell asleep or fainted."

She nodded. "Your records indicate a history of SVT, and your blood sugar is really low based on your blood sample. Your pulse was out of whack when the EMTs first checked it."

"Fuck." I rolled my head to the side. "I've been trying to go slow with this medication. I wanted to take the lowest dose possible, but I guess I'll have to adjust it."

"Maybe talk to your doctor. You're lucky."

"How am I lucky?"

"Well, it could have been a lot worse. Nobody else was on the road nearby when it happened. You're lucky someone drove by right afterward. It looks like you ran into the guardrail, and your car bounced to the other side and then rolled down an embankment."

Having it spelled out like that made my stomach drop. "Lucky, I guess so."

"We're going to do a scan to rule out internal bleeding. Then stitch this up." She gestured toward my shoulder, which was throbbing like hell. "One of the EMTs spoke to your brother and someone else out at the place where you live, someone named Daphne," she said, looking down at a computer screen. "Apparently, you already have people waiting to see you."

"Oh wow," I murmured.

"It's good to have people who care," she offered with a quick smile.

Fortunately, I had no internal bleeding. Quinn happened to be the doctor on duty. He numbed my shoulder before he stitched the gash. He gave me some painkillers even though I wanted to argue the point. Helen had said, "You're going to be hurting like hell tonight when you get home, so take them."

When I was all ready to go, he smiled down at me. "Let me guess, you took a red-eye flight back to Anchorage, didn't sleep, probably didn't eat, and decided it was just the time to drive back."

I glared at him. "Maybe."

"You'll be able to keep your driver's license, but we need to adjust that medication."

"Are you sure I fainted? I could've just fallen asleep," I insisted.

"You fainted. I read the reports. Your heartbeat was still erratic when the EMTs arrived."

I sighed. "Fine. I will succumb to your recommendations."

He chuckled. "Good. You ready for some visitors? You can have two at a time."

"How much longer am I going to be here?" I wanted out. Now.

"I'd like you to stay at least another two hours for observation."

"It's late, though. Can I just go home?"

"You can, but that would be against medical advice."

"Fine," I muttered.

"Give it a few minutes, and we'll send the visitors back."

I wasn't sure who was even here waiting. I figured Diego would be here. More than anything, I wanted to see Grant. I felt silly and foolish. I'd been in such a rush to get to him that I almost killed myself in the process. I thought about my sister's observations about my stubbornness. I pressed my lips together and let out a big sigh.

No matter what Grant said or how he felt, I wanted to tell him how I felt. Even though it terrified me.

There was a light knock on the door before Helen peered in. "You get one visitor first, VIP."

She swung the door open and winked just before Grant walked in, and my heart went crazy. He stopped a few feet inside the door. I heard a soft whisper of air as it closed behind him. My heart felt unsteady again, and I heard the monitor beeping. I prayed no one would come in to check on me. It was bad enough that I was about to fall apart in front of Grant. I didn't need an audience.

His eyes held mine from across the room. In several long strides, he reached the side of my bed. I hadn't even noticed that my hands were cold until he curled one of his over my hand, and the warmth of his touch was a contrast to the icy cold.

"Harley, you're freezing," he said.

Before I could even open my mouth to say anything, the door opened again, and Helen was back. "I thought for a minute there you might be running a marathon," she said lightly as she approached.

"I'm just nervous," I croaked. I was mortified when I felt hot tears spill down my cheeks.

"She's freezing," Grant said.

Helen nodded. "I have just the thing." She spun around quickly, going through another doorway in my room and reappearing with a blanket. "Here's a heated one."

I nodded as I sniffled. She laid it over me, and the radiant warmth was an instant relief. "Oh, that feels good." I smeared my free hand over my nose.

Helen, clearly taking pity on me, tugged several tissues out of the box on the small tray beside my bed and handed them to me. She looked over at Grant. "It's normal for people to feel emotional after an accident. It's discombobulating."

Grant nodded. "Thank you."

She left the room quickly. Grant released my hand, and I felt bereft, but he adjusted the blanket, tucking it more snugly around me. "You need to get warm. What happened?" he asked.

My throat ached with emotion, and my thoughts were a jumble, but one point of clarity rose through the cacophony. "I love you," I said hoarsely.

He was quiet for just long enough that my heartbeat started to speed up again. This time in anxiety and fear that I'd made a mistake in telling him how I felt. Not that I believed anyone deserved to have someone return their feelings, but no one wanted to be rejected. Especially not me.

"I love you too," he said, his voice low and his gaze intent.

There went my next round of tears. He looked around wildly before he spied a chair nearby. He tugged it close and sat down as he reached for the box of tissues and handed me a few more.

I dabbed at my eyes and blew my nose, mumbling. "I'm sorry."

"For what?"

I rolled my eyes. Sarcasm could always help me find my composure. I lifted my hands up as the tears raced down my cheeks.

"Hey, Helen just said that's normal."

"I'm not crying because I had an accident." I sniffled.

"Well, maybe you are," he said softly. He reached up and brushed my hair off my forehead, smoothing it back. "I missed you."

I swallowed, my throat loosening. "I missed you too." I blew my nose again. "Wow. I suck at reunions," I offered with a little laugh. I dabbed at my tears with the balled-up tissue.

He shrugged. "Is anybody good at them?"

"Well, you're not crying."

As he stared back at me, I realized he had a sheen of tears in his eyes. He rested his hand over mine, still tucked under the blanket, and squeezed gently. "I should have told you I would be out of town for two weeks."

"You didn't have to go," I pointed out, laughing as soon as I said that because I was being contrary and stubborn.

"No, I didn't."

I took a shaky breath, relieved I seemed to have my tears under control. "I didn't call you back because I wanted to come back early and surprise you. I heard you got attacked by a bear."

"Who told you that?"

"Daphne. Are you okay?"

This time, he rolled his eyes. "Pretty much. I'll have some nice scars on my leg. It hurt like hell when it happened, but I'm fine."

There went my tears again. So much for playing it cool. I reached for another tissue and blew my nose.

Chapter Thirty-Five

GRANT

Harley swiped at her cheeks with her palms, and I passed over some more tissues. My throat was knotted with emotion, and my chest hurt.

"Are you okay?"

She sniffled, blinking rapidly as she lifted her gaze to mine. "Uh-huh, but you got attacked by a bear," she wailed before bursting into another round of noisy tears.

This was the first time a woman had cried like this in front of me. Although I had two sisters, they were more prone to losing their tempers than bursting into tears.

"I'm fine," I insisted. "I swear. You want to see my leg?"

She shook her head quickly when I stood to jokingly unbutton my jeans. "Grant!" she yelped just as the door opened, and Helen peered in again.

She pinned her gaze on me. "You need to stop getting her heart going. That's what caused this in the first place."

I looked down at Harley and back at Helen before

I sat down quickly. "Sorry." Helen disappeared again. "What is she talking about?" I asked, fully aware Harley had yet to explain what happened.

"You know I've been dealing with that heart issue," she began. She twisted a tissue between her fingers.

"Yeah, but you were taking your medication. Are you okay?"

"Quinn said he needs to adjust the dose. But when I heard you got hurt, I kind of panicked. I took an early flight back. I didn't eat much on the flight, and I couldn't sleep. After I landed, I was tired, but I wanted to get here, so I started driving. Quinn told me I just can't be casual about things like that. Based on the monitoring info from the EMT's, he thinks I fainted, which caused the accident. I'm sorry," she whispered hoarsely.

My eyes stung with tears. I reached for one of her hands, holding it between mine and stroking my thumb across her wrist, where I could feel the steady beat of her pulse. I almost needed to feel it. I needed the reassurance.

"You don't have to apologize. I get it. Maybe I overreacted because of what happened with my mom—"

Her hair swung as she shook her head quickly. "You didn't. I've been annoyed about it, and I guess in denial."

"You? Avoiding something?" I managed to tease lightly.

She rolled her eyes, squeezing one of my hands. "I guess I've always needed to be tough. I got defensive when I should have been smart. I was in a hurry to get back and see you, but I should have stopped and gotten something to eat. Now, I'm being honest with you about this, so for God's sake, don't drive me crazy over it."

The vulnerability in her eyes nearly undid me. My heart swelled, and I smiled down at her, joy punching its fist through the fear inside my heart. "As if that would work," I said.

She looked chagrined. "Lesson learned. It's possible I just fell asleep, but I'm lucky nobody else was on that stretch of road when it happened. Someone came by right after it happened, which is why the EMTs got there so fast. My car bounced and rolled, but I'm fine."

"Are you fine, though?" I pressed.

"I mean, I'll be sore, but all things considered, yes."

Quiet fell between us. I kept brushing my thumb over the steady beat of her pulse on the inside of her wrist. A moment later, I leaned over, brushing my lips over hers. I meant for it to be a chaste kiss.

But she arched closer, making a soft sound at the back of her throat. Her tongue darted out to glide against mine. The next thing I knew, that monitor was beeping again. We broke apart just before Helen opened the door.

"She's one hell of a chaperone," I murmured.

Harley giggled and sniffled again.

Chapter Thirty-Six

HARLEY

The following day, Daphne waved a hand airily in the direction of the table in the front of the kitchen. "Sit," she ordered.

When I let out a sigh, Daphne narrowed her eyes. "Are you actually going to argue with me about this? You just had a car accident."

I felt my cheeks heat as I rolled my eyes. "Fine," I muttered under my breath.

Cat called after me, "We're going to pamper you and drive you insane."

When I laughed, my sore shoulder twinged with pain. My own stubbornness and insistence had gotten me into this mess. The most annoying part was that I had started to come to terms with my heart condition. I'd just been in a rush to get back to Grant.

I sat down at the table in my preferred corner. In my opinion, it offered the best view. Although when it came to views at the lodge, that was splitting hairs. To one side was the evergreen forest with a pretty stand of birch along the sloping hill. In another month or so, the grassy field would be awash in pink from the fireweed that covered the open fields of Alaska, offering vista after vista of flowers. Fireweed was the precursor to autumn here and offered more color than autumn did, which was mostly golds and coppers.

Kachemak Bay glittered in the distance, and beyond that, Mount Augustine stood quiet in the inlet, a tall, silent volcano rising out of the ocean. I kept telling myself that someday I would go out there. I was so curious, but that would be for another day.

I reflexively started to turn when I heard Cat say something and then winced. She wagged a finger at me. "See? You need to be careful with your shoulder." She set the platter she held in her other hand down beside me.

"What's this?" I asked.

"Take a bite and guess. It's like a box of chocolates."

"Except it's not a box of chocolates," I pointed out.

She grinned. "I know, but they all have different fillings."

"Ooh, what are my options?"

"You're just going to have to be surprised."

"Thank God, I trust you and Daphne. I'm not the most adventurous eater."

"You're not?" Cat prompted.

"I'd call myself average. But it wouldn't be for just anyone that I would try something if I didn't know what was inside." The rolls were fluffy with a shiny surface. "What makes them shiny?" I asked as I lifted one.

"It's how I proved the dough," Daphne called over.

"I don't know what that means," I said as I glanced up at Cat.

She grinned and circled her hand in the air, clearly impatient for me to try one. I took a bite.

Flavor broke across my tongue, savory with a hint of sweetness, cheese, and spinach. "Cheese and something sweet with spinach?"

Cat's grin widened. "Can you guess the cheese?"

I took another bite to be sure. "Brie," I announced.

She clapped her hands. "What else?"

"Spinach, and, I don't know, something sweet is in there."

"Brown sugar. Sugar makes everything better," Daphne offered.

I finished the roll and glanced at Cat. "You know we still haven't had the card night."

She shrugged. "I know. I got busy with the play. It'll be over after the next two weekends, so let's make it happen."

A few minutes later, I felt Grant's presence before I saw him when a prickling sensation skittered up my spine and heat suffused me. Honestly, even though I had accepted my feelings for him, it was embarrassing to have a man affect me this easily and powerfully.

I glanced over my shoulder. He had paused by the counter and was saying something to Flynn, who must have come in with him. Whether or not he sensed my eyes on him, he paused midsentence and glanced in my direction. His lips kicked up at the corners before he looked back toward Flynn, cuffing him lightly on the shoulder and then crossing over to where I sat at the table. Flynn's gaze followed him, pausing to meet mine. He winked before turning to drop a kiss on Daphne's cheek.

Grant slipped into the chair beside me, immediately asking, "How do you feel?"

"I feel like I'm tired of people asking me how I feel," I replied.

Unruffled, Grant shrugged. "Deal with it. That's what people do when they give a shit."

What would have once annoyed me only elicited a giggle now. "How do you feel?" I glanced down at his thigh, although his jeans covered his injury.

"It's itchy," he offered.

"That's a good sign. It means it's healing."

I felt too good to fuss and simply leaned back in my chair, savoring the feel of his arm sliding across my shoulders.

"Am I allowed to kiss you in front of everybody?"

My cheeks were burning up, and I glanced over my shoulder. "Yes, but don't make a show."

"I know you'll never be into PDA," he murmured before he quickly leaned over and dusted a kiss on the side of my neck.

Goose bumps chased over my skin. My entire body felt fizzy and sparkly. Dear God, how in the world was I actually going to live with this man? Well, I already did live with him, so that was convenient.

Hours later, we were back at the staff house. It was just Grant and me.

"When does Cat's play start?" I asked.

"You mean the actual performances?" Grant stretched his legs out, resting his feet on the coffee table. At my nod, he added, "I'm not sure, but I think next weekend. I should know this."

"I don't," I offered with a shrug.

"Honestly, I wouldn't mind if this play went on for months."

"Yeah?" I tucked my feet under my knees as I leaned back into the corner of the couch.

He glanced over, replying, "Hell yeah. It means we have the house to ourselves. Also..." He leaned over, snaking his long arm around my waist and tugging me close to his side. "You're not close enough."

I burst out laughing. He shifted closer with his arm tightening around my waist and his lips maybe an inch from mine when he spoke. "So, what should we do with all this privacy?"

My belly felt light and fluttery, and my breath was short. "I don't know. You're injured."

"So are you," he pointed out.

We'd actually had a teasing argument about who was technically more injured last night. I thought it was Grant because he had more stitches. Whereas he thought it was me because I was in a car accident, which he said was more dramatic than a bear attack. I felt pressed to rehash the debate again. "I just want to point out I don't think a car accident is more dramatic than a bear attack."

His breath gusted against my neck when he laughed softly just before he nipped the sensitive skin there. I shivered against him.

"Why do you say that?" He lifted his head, his eyes holding mine.

"Because car accidents are common. Getting attacked by a bear is definitely not," I pointed out.

"I don't know if I would call it an attack," he clarified. "She just swiped my leg."

"Oh my God, what is it with you people in Alaska?"

"What do you mean?"

"You act like it's not a big deal, and you have stitches from a bear!"

"I'm fine. More people get injured in moose encounters every year in Alaska. I was probably in more danger when you chased that moose off."

"Wow, you are such a man."

"I am, in fact, a man," he offered lightly. His gaze sobered. "I promise, I'm fine," he whispered just before dipping his head and claiming my mouth in a bold, commanding kiss.

Grant's kisses were my downfall. Ever since the first one, I'd fallen so hard. I was breathless by the time he lifted his head.

My heart was drumming rapidly, and I sucked in a breath. "We can't do this right here," I murmured.

"What do you mean? We have the house to ourselves."

Before I could debate further, he lifted me carefully, setting me on my feet and undressing me as if he were unwrapping a present.

I was shivering with anticipation by the time he stood and kicked his jeans aside. Even though I'd seen it last night, I still gasped when I looked down at his thigh. Deep marks marred the surface. The stitches were tidy.

"Don't worry about it," he said. I looked up at him. "You worry about you, and I'll worry about me. Now, where were we?"

Seconds later, he was sitting down, and I was straddling him. The position was the best option for both of us. My shoulder was sore, but I didn't have to worry about twisting or shifting too much.

When I felt the slow, delicious slide of him filling me, I got lost in his dark eyes.

"I love you," he whispered.

EPILOGUE

Grant

"I'm so excited!" Harley whisper-shouted beside me.

She squeezed my hand where her fingers were laced with mine on the armrest between our seats in the small theater. I grinned. "Same here. I hope it goes well. Cat seemed nervous."

"I know," Daphne said, leaning around Harley to glance at me. "She said she's nervous because it's her first play."

"She's going to kill it," Nora commented from behind us. "I know she's a good actress."

"How do you know that?" Flynn asked, leaning behind Daphne to look at Nora.

"Because she was such a dramatic kid growing up." Nora deadpanned.

Harley giggled. "I can actually see that."

We were all here—Diego and Gemma were to one side of me, Daphne and Flynn were on the other side of Harley, Elias and Cammi were behind us with Nora and Gabriel beside them, and Skylar and Tucker on the other side. Cat had complained that we used up all of her comp tickets, so Flynn had decided to buy tickets for all of us. Cat was later mortified because she discovered we were all sitting in the first two rows. However, she had happily handed out her comp tickets to her friends.

The lights began to dim, and we all fell quiet. When the curtain opened, I was nervous for my little sister. She'd been working so hard on this, but she was incredible and even brought tears to my eyes. There was a standing ovation at the end. Daphne had arranged for flowers to be delivered to her from us.

We circled around Cat after the performance. She was beaming, not even making a sarcastic comment when I gave her a hug and whispered, "You kicked ass," in her ear.

She stepped back and smiled at Harley and me. "I don't have practice tonight, but I'm going to stay for the after-party. Is that okay?"

Flynn chuckled, clapping me on the shoulder when Cat turned away. "Of course, it's okay. You get the house to yourself again. If you didn't know it, you're in love," he pointed out.

I was, and I didn't even care who teased me about it.

Later that night, Harley said, "We should wait up for Cat." When I asked her why, she looked over at me. "Because this is her first live play performance. It's a big deal."

I took that to mean I needed to hurry and teased her until she was blushing. When we heard the sound of the door opening, Harley rolled off my lap so fast I burst out laughing.

Cat came in, her eyes widening when she saw us. She glanced at the TV, which was on even though we weren't watching it. "What did you wait up for?"

Harley stood, crossing the room and giving her a big hug. When she stepped back, she squeezed Cat's shoulders. "To congratulate you again because you were amazing."

"Really?"

"Absolutely."

"I'm glad you're going to be my sister-in-law," Cat replied.

Harley's eyes went wide with shock on her face. Maybe I hadn't asked her yet, but I was planning to marry Harley. I needed to make sure she understood she was everything I wanted.

When she looked over at me, I shrugged. "Maybe now's not the best time, but you know you're forever for me."

Cat squealed, and Harley's eyes nearly bugged out of her face before tears spilled down her cheeks. I leaped up from the couch. "Hey." She shook her head as I said, "I didn't mean to upset you."

"You didn't. I'm just…" Her words ended with a sniffle.

I wrapped her in my arms. "Hey, I was just teasing. I mean, not really, but—"

She peered up at me. "The answer is yes."

Cat squealed again. "I love that this happened in front of me," she said a moment later after Harley had swiped the tears away from her eyes and blown her nose.

"Why?" I asked.

"Because we're all roommates, and you were sneaking around for what felt like forever. You might as well propose in front of me. I knew it before you two even got together." With that, she flounced up the stairs calling, "Good night! I'm exhausted."

A little while later, I lay in bed, sliding my fingers

through Harley's hair. She traced circles on my chest, saying softly, "You know we can wait."

"I know we can wait, but I see no point in not being honest about how I feel."

Her luminous green eyes held mine. "Wow," she whispered.

Thank you for reading Harley & Grant's story! Want a glimpse of the future for them? Join my newsletter to receive an exclusive scene.

Sign up here: https://BookHip.com/DRDTTQF

p.s. If you are already subscribed, you'll still be able to access the scene.

My upcoming release is With Every Breath in the Light My Fire Series.

Alice's return home to Alaska all starts with putting on an accidental skinny-dipping show for a wedding party. Oops.

Jonah happens to be Alice's new neighbor, and the first time he sees her she's naked. Well then.

Jonah came to Alaska to escape painful memories. He considers himself damaged goods and not fit for romance. He didn't plan on Alice. He didn't plan on the fire blazing to life between them.

Don't miss Alice & Jonah's story - it's emotional, sexy, sweet and full of heart & soul!

Pre-order With Every Breath - due out Oct 11, 2022!

For more swoony romance...

This Crazy Love kicks off the Swoon Series - small town southern romance with enough heat to melt you! Jackson & Shay's story is epic - swoon-worthy & intensely emotional. Jackson just happens to be Shay's brother's best friend. He's also *seriously* easy on the eyes. Shay has a past, the kind of past she would most definitely like to forget. Past or not, Jackson is about to rock her world. Don't miss their story! Free on all retailers!

Burn For Me is a second chance romance for the ages. Sexy firefighters? Check. Rugged men? Check. Wrapped up together? Check. Brave the fire in this hot, small-town romance. Amelia & Cade were high school sweethearts & then it all fell apart. When they cross paths again, it's epic - don't miss Cade's story! Free on all retailers!

For more small town romance, take a visit to Last Frontier Lodge in Diamond Creek. A sexy, alpha SEAL meets his match with a brainy heroine in Take Me Home. Marley is all brains & Gage is all brawn. Sparks fly when their worlds collide. Don't miss Gage & Marley's story! Free on all retailers!

If sports romance lights your spark, check out The Play. Liam is a British footballer who falls for Olivia, his doctor. A twist of forbidden heats up this swoon-worthy & laugh-out-loud romance. Don't miss Liam & Olivia's story.

Free on all retailers!

Visit my store to purchase ebooks & fun swag!
J.H. Croix Shop
Light My Fire Series
Wild With You
Hold Me Now
Only Ever Us
Fall For Me
Keep Me Close
With Every Breath - coming Oct 2022!
Dare With Me Series
Crash Into You
Evers & Afters
Come To Me
Back To Us
Take Me There
After We Fall
Swoon Series
This Crazy Love
Wait For Me
Break My Fall
Truly Madly Mine
Still Go Crazy
If We Dare
Steal My Heart
Into The Fire Series
Burn For Me
Slow Burn
Burn So Bad
Hot Mess
Burn So Good
Sweet Fire
Play With Fire
Melt With You
Burn For You
Crash & Burn

That Snowy Night

Brit Boys Sports Romance

The Play

Big Win

Out Of Bounds

Play Me

Naughty Wish

Diamond Creek Alaska Novels

When Love Comes

Follow Love

Love Unbroken

Love Untamed

Tumble Into Love

Christmas Nights

Last Frontier Lodge Novels

Take Me Home

Love at Last

Just This Once

Falling Fast

Stay With Me

When We Fall

Hold Me Close

Crazy For You

Just Us

ACKNOWLEDGMENTS

Hugs & more hugs to my readers. You all kick ass. Thank you for reading & cheering on my stories time and again!

Much gratitude to my editor, to Terri D. for proofreading, and to my early readers for catching those stubborn errors.

Gracious thanks to Najla Qamber for the stunning covers for this series and for her patience with me.

To all the bloggers, bookstagrammers, and booktokers who shout out their love of romance stories - mine and so many more.

My assistant works the scenes in the background and makes sure I only forget the things I forget to tell her about.

To DBC and our dogs: I love you.

xoxo
J.H. Croix